# BEAUTY

*Learning to Live A Devil's Blaze Duet Book 2*

# JORDAN MARIE

# COPYRIGHT

Cover Art by Letitia Hasser RBA Cover Designs
Models: Connor Smith & Jocii Navarrete
Photographer: Reggie Deanching R plus M Photo

# WARNING:

This book contains sexual situations, violence and other adult themes. Recommended for 18 and above. This book may also contain emotional triggers. Please read with caution.

# BEAUTY: LEARNING TO LIVE

Book 2 of
A Devil's Blaze Duet

By:

Jordan Marie

# BLURB

**This isn't your everyday Beauty and the Beast story.**
**Our love story was tragic, until it wasn't....**
Once upon a time I fell in love with a beast.
I fell fast.
I fell hard.
I loved him intensely and I trusted him completely - until he
ripped my heart to shreds.
Love isn't a fairy tale.
It's messy.
It's dirty.
It's painful, and it's ugly.
Until it's not....

# DEDICATION

*To my beautiful Jordan, my angel. When I began writing, I wanted you with me. Our names linked as I embarked upon a journey I had always wanted, but had given up the dream of achieving. I let other people dictate what I did, how I lived. I let them bind my wings. Somehow I overcame that, and you were there with me. Now 16 books later, I have you in my heart and I feel like my wings are spread and some days I truly soar. One day I will soar home to you. I love you.*

*--Mom*

# PROLOGUE

## HAYDEN

I run blindly from the barn. My mind is swirling in so many directions, I don't know what I'm doing. All I know is that I need to get away from Michael. The hateful and cruel things he said left me feeling like I'm bleeding and raw, only the wound is on the inside. A wound that goes all the way into my soul...my spirit. I don't know how to process all of the things Michael just threw at me. I don't know how I feel about them.

I run into the house, taking the time to lock the door and then I go straight to my room. I find my suitcase and open it on the bed, throwing things into it without a rhyme or reason. I have to get away. I can't stay here. I *won't* count on his protection against Blade. I can't stay near Michael. I'm on my own. My hand trembles as I go to hold my stomach. *Maggie and I* are on our own. I go to the drawer in my dresser that I've been putting away special items for Maggie and carefully pack those too. It's not much, but it's something. On my way out of the house I stop by her nursery. My heart hurts as I look at it. The furniture, the lamp, the bedding... it's all perfect, made to make a child happy, made to make a child feel loved and like she has a home. I look at the glider, and I hate that more tears fall. Tears that had just begun to stop, now run down my face unchecked again. I hate Michael for tearing apart my dreams. I...*hate him*. I pull myself away from the room and force myself to leave. I know I only have two options at this point. If it was just me, I'd take off driving and try and start over. It's not smart, but my trust in others is gone completely at this point. I don't trust Michael not to come and find me when he sobers up. I don't trust Blade not to find me either. I have to be smart. Maggie is depending on me. I'm all she has. *She's all I have.* I reach in my pocket and pull out the cellphone that Michael bought me. It has two numbers programmed into it. I choose the one I want, ignoring the sick feeling when I see Michael's name. I definitely won't need that number again.

"Hello?" the voice answers. I clear my throat as nerves assault me.

"Mr.... Mr. Torasani. It's Hayden...Hayden Graham."

"Hayden are you okay? Where is Mr. Jameson?"

"I...I'm okay. I can't explain right now, but I know you offered to take me back to your home for safety. If the offer is still open, I was wondering if I could come out there. If that's okay, I mean. I just...I need to get away and I need my daughter to be safe."

"What about your friend Mr. Jameson?"

"He's part of the reason I need to get away. Listen, maybe this was a bad idea. Just forget I called. I'll be okay—"

"I'll have Clive there in a couple of minutes."

"A couple of minutes?" I squeak.

"I've had him and some others watching you. I may have had to go home, but I didn't leave you unprotected," he says and shock runs through me at the revelation. I listen as he describes Clive to me, so I won't be worried when he shows up. I hang up the phone, stunned. I walk to the door and just like Victor said, there's a knock at the door within just a few minutes. I fight down even more nerves. *No more panic attacks.* I'll get therapy, I'll do whatever I need to do, but I will not allow myself to be weak again. This will be the last time I depend on anyone for help. I will be strong for Maggie. I put my phone on the kitchen table. I won't be needing that ever again. I'm leaving it behind.

*Just like I'm leaving Michael behind.*

# PROLOGUE

## BEAST

*(One Month Later)*

"Damn Sunshine, you look like shit," Devil's voice grates from behind me. I close my eyes, stopping my axe mid swing. I turn to look over my shoulder at the asshole. I grunt at him and then turn back around to smash the axe into the waiting wood. "Always so welcoming. Is it any wonder you've been living out here by yourself, rotting away?" Devil adds, proving he's not going to just disappear.

"Get the fuck out of here," I growl. I don't want company. I've told Diesel that. I've told Dani and Crusher that. I've even told Skull and Beth that when they decided to come visit. I don't want any of them here. Devil's not wrong. I am rotting away, but then that's what I want.

"So sweet. Do you kiss your mother with that mouth?" he jokes, and this time when the axe strikes the wood, I might be imagining it is his head.

"No, but you should see the shit I've done to your mother with it."

"Probably. My mother is a whore. You might want to get tested," Devil jokes with a laugh. The laugh only gets louder when I flip him off.

"What are you doing here?" I ask, propping up another piece of wood to split.

"Skull found a lead about your woman, and though he told me you weren't interested anymore, I thought I'd take a chance. You know, on the off chance that you've managed to pull your head out of your ass."

"I don't have any interest in Hayden anymore. She's gone," I tell him, lying through my teeth. I miss her smile, her laugh and her eyes. I really miss her eyes. I miss the way they used to shine with happiness, or glow with need when I was driving into her body. My hands shake like some coke-head going through withdrawals, which is essentially what I am. Still, I don't need Devil or anyone to update me about Hayden. I know she's safe. I've kept in touch with Victor this past month. The only difference is that now she is hiding from me as well as Blade.

"I wonder how many times a day you say that shit? Have you been able to make yourself believe it yet?" he asks, sitting on an old stump across from me. I grab another piece of wood and split it with my axe, before finally responding.

"Is there a reason you're here busting my balls?" I ask him, taking a break and using the handle of the axe as a cane to lean on. I'm dead tired. I've been splitting wood since daybreak and it's now almost two in the afternoon. I don't need the wood, I'm just that frustrated.

"Skull sent this to Diesel. He said your stubborn ass might want to see it."

"I told you I don't have a fucking thing to do with Hayden anymore. That part of my life is over—*dead and gone*," I tell him, and the words cause that open wound inside of me to hurt again. It's hurt every day I've been without Hayden—and it's only getting worse.

"Oh," Devil says taking out a well-worn folded piece of paper and holding it loosely between two of his fingers. "I guess Diesel was right when he said you wouldn't want to know that Hayden was on the move again," he adds, waving the paper around.

"He was right," I lie. I want to yank that fucking piece of paper out of his hands. She can't be on the move. Victor would have told me...he would have told me if she was leaving Boston.

Devil is watching me. I know he is, because I can feel his eyes on me. They're burning a hole through me. I try to pretend like I'm busy sifting through the small cooler sitting beside me. I grab a beer and open it, guzzling it down, while trying to block him out. When I hear the crinkling of paper, I can't stop myself from turning around. I do my best not to flinch, but I don't think I fully succeed. When Devil smirks, I'm positive. He takes his eyes off of me for a quick minute and then takes aim. I watch as he tosses the paper into a large bucket by the wall of the barn. The bucket is overflowing with rain water because it stormed all night. I resist the urge to yank the paper out of there, before the information can't be read. *It's not easy.*

"Too bad. I hate to think of poor Hayden all alone in a hospital room."

"Hospital?" I roughly exhale the word, because it suddenly feels like I can't breathe. Victor promised me he was keeping her safe and that he would let me know the minute Blade showed up. Did Blade get to her? Did he hurt her when I wasn't there to keep her safe? *Had I failed Maggie, just like I failed Annabelle?*

"Checked her in yesterday. She was having contractions."

"Contractions? But she's not due yet."

"Some women go early. Or so I'm told. I know next to fucking nothing about that—*thank God,*" he laughs. I ignore him, walking over and grabbing the now soaked paper. I unkink the wrinkles in it, trying to unfold it. Devil is laughing his ass off at me. I vow when I get this damn paper fixed, I'm going to deck him. If only to stop that fucking annoying laugh of his.

"Shut the fuck up," I growl, still trying to pull the corners of the folded paper apart.

"For a man who doesn't care about the girl—"

"I don't," I growl.

"A girl who is dead and gone to him," he adds. I hate that he even associates those words with Hayden.

"I said my life with her is dead and gone. That book has closed. She's moved on and so have I."

"To what? Your love affair with an axe? Jesus, Beast I haven't seen this much wood since that time Diesel rented that male-on-male, gangbang porn flick for Crusher's bachelor party."

"What the fuck did he do that for?"

"Dani paid him to."

"Christ she's twisted."

"You aren't lying. Shit, I had to fuck ten different women before visions of bobbing dicks stopped appearing when I closed my eyes."

"I bet that was a rough few days for you," I gripe, more concerned about the paper I can't get to pull apart than the fact that Devil was haunted by images of dicks.

"Days? Fuck no. I fucked them all together. Hell of a party. Poor dick was sore for days," he laughs and I'm pretty sure he's not joking. He's got a tattoo of the numbers 666 above his dick. It's how he got his road name, the Devil. His crew swears he had to have sold his soul to use his dick as much as he does.

"This fucking paper is blank," I snarl, when the damn thing finally unfolds.

"I know," Devil shrugs. "The paper with the hospital information is in my pocket," he adds, pulling it out and handing it to me. I grab it, giving him a look that should make a man quake in fear. The bastard just cackles that annoying laugh again.

"Then what the fuck was the point of all that?"

"Just wanted to prove something to you," he shrugs.

"What?" I ask distracted, because I'm reading the address.

"You're a fucking mess man. You're about as fun to be around as a whore with no teeth, warts and a flared case of herpes."

"Christ."

"But at least when Hayden was around, you had potential. I

don't know what all your damage is. It's not my place to know. But seems to me if you are stuck on this earth, you might as well make the most of it."

"You don't know shit," I mutter.

"Maybe not. But I'll tell you what I do know."

"What's that?" I ask, not looking at him and instead staring at the paper in my hand.

"Your ass is going to be flying out to Boston in the morning. And I think that says pretty clearly that Hayden means something to you. A man—a smart *man* would think long and hard on that before he pisses it away. *If he hasn't already.*" He doesn't understand. He doesn't know about my past. He doesn't know how sweet and giving Hayden is. If he did he would understand that she deserves more than what I could give her.

"She deserves better," I murmur to myself, not really to Devil.

"Maybe she's already found it. She's the type of woman that makes a man want to step up to the plate."

"She's pregnant," I argue, not liking the idea of other men vying for Hayden's attention. I never thought about that, and I don't like it.

"That wouldn't matter to some men—they might even like it. Hell, Sunshine, if you don't want her, maybe I'll see how she likes the Ole' Devil. I could use some good in my life."

"Stay the fuck away from her," I growl, walking away from him.

"Where you going?" he calls from behind me.

"I'm going to pack."

"Aren't you going to offer me a beer?"

"Go fuck yourself," I answer, slamming the door on his fucking laugh.

## 1

### BEAST

I f there is a definition of Hell on Earth this would be at least one form of it. Seeing the woman who haunts you, watching her, wanting her and yet never being able to have her. This has been my life for two months. *Two long fucking months.*

At first, I followed Hayden to Boston. I left the day Devil told me she was having contractions. I wasn't able to see her, there was no way I could without letting her know I was there. I knew that's the last thing she wanted, and she didn't need the extra stress. Victor kept me updated. Hell, we were sharing a drink when he told me that Hayden was suffering from some kind of fake contractions, not real ones—something called Braxton Hicks. I was relieved, but even when she was released from the hospital, I stayed close by. The moment Victor told me Hayden was moving....

It is all a blur, but that's why I'm sitting outside the home Victor set Hayden up in—a home that just happens to be in Wyoming. When Victor called me two days after Hayden left North Carolina, I was a fucking mess. I could only remember bits and pieces of that night in the loft. I remembered enough to know I'd finally pushed her away, which was needed. I was dreaming. I can't be the man that Hayden deserves. She needs someone better. And me? I deserve nothing. For a minute Hayden made me believe I could live again, I could have a life...I could be *happy*.

*Who the fuck did I think I was? What made me think I could go on living, when I'm essentially the one who killed my daughter? The daughter I wasn't man enough to protect. The daughter I wasn't man enough to save. The daughter I fucking forgot existed while I sunk my dick inside Hayden. What was I doing? Was I trying to replace Annabelle with Hayden's daughter? Fuck. Am I that twisted?*

For months those same questions have been haunting me, just like the memory of Hayden's body. Just like the sound of Hayden laughing, of her whispering my name, of that little breathy gasp she makes when I touch that spot that sends her over the edge...

Christ, I feel like the memories of her are eating me alive. I feel like a cat on a hot tin roof, everything inside of me jumping around, never settling, as if any minute I'll jump out of my own fucking skin. I need to just let her go. I know I need to, but every time I try to do it, I remember that Blade is out there. That Hayden is pregnant and that I pledged to take care of Maggie. I can't fail her like I did Annabelle. *I can't.*

So...I've followed her around like an idiot, making sure she's safe. Which is why I'm still here. Sitting outside in the rain, watching through the window as Hayden brushes her hair. I'm like some perverted peeping Tom. Looking at what I want through the window. What I want, but should never have. My hand literally shakes as I reach up and touch my beard. My fingers finding the deepest groove of the scars hidden beneath and rubbing back and forth against it—a calming reminder that I'm not human. *Not anymore.*

I watch as Hayden's head goes down. Her dark hair fans out around her face, hiding the beauty that is her underneath it. She's got one hand on her stomach, sitting there at her vanity and you don't have to be clairvoyant to know she's crying. The sadness radiates from her, reaching out to me—even through the distance. Guilt hits me, because I know I'm at least part of the reason for these tears. My eyes automatically move to the living room window. That's where Victor's man is. Clive Stroker. I hate the fucker. I don't even know him, but I hate that he's living with Hayden, even if it is for her protection. I hate that he gets her laughs. I hate that he's the one to make her smile. I hate that I've seen him hold her fucking hand. And, as fucked up as it sounds, I hate Hayden for letting him hold her hand. The hand that I held when she gave herself to me. The hand that I held when I claimed her and Maggie...*my hand.*

It's a wonder I'm not fucking mad with the twisted thoughts that keep running through my head. Then again, I'm sitting outside in the pouring rain, watching the woman I pushed away, cursing the fact that someone else is in my spot.

*That has to be the very definition of crazy.*

## 2

# HAYDEN

That feeling is back again. The one of being watched. I rake the back of my hand against my cheeks, trying to erase the evidence of my tears. Tears are for the weak, and that's not who I am—not anymore. I don't need a mantra. I'm not the woman I was when Michael first met me. I'm not even the woman who ran out of his barn loft two months ago. I've changed. I've gotten stronger—*I survived*.

A large part of that is Victor. He saved me that night. He took me in, and then he helped me move to Wyoming. I don't know why I picked Wyoming. I spent days thinking about it. Something about the irony of moving to a town that was actually called Nowhere, Wyoming appealed to me. God knows it feels like my life had been going nowhere for way too long. He helped me get financing for an already established bakery—his only condition was I rename it Charlie's—which I would have anyway. He insisted that I live in this house and that Clive watch over me. It may have been weak to agree to all of that, but without him, I never would have been able to do it. The truth was, I needed to put as many miles as I could between me and Michael. I gave him a month.

One month I stayed in Boston with Victor, and in that month, I didn't hear one word from Michael. I don't know what I would have said or done if I had. I just know the fact that I didn't hear from him hurt and it also cemented the fact that it was truly over. That acceptance was the kick in the ass that I needed. I decided it was way past time to get my life in order. Victor helped me, reluctantly. Neither one of us felt that Blade's reach would find me in Wyoming. The man was never that smart, plus his resources are nothing now. Still, Victor wanted me to be safe, and he felt the best way to achieve that was to stay with him. When I refused, he gave in, but only because he knew Clive would protect me. I wanted to object, but Maggie had to come first—so I agreed. I don't know what I will do after Maggie is born. If I still haven't heard from Blade, then it will be time to start focusing on my life as Maggie's mother—*alone*. I'm not sure how Victor, *or Clive,* will react to that.

I take a breath, get up and walk to the window. It's storming again. Something that rarely happens this time of year. I'm told Nowhere is normally dry as dust right now, but in the four weeks that I've lived here, it's been rain, rain and more rain. Lightning flashes through the sky, highlighting the back yard. I cry out when I see a large figure outside wearing a black poncho, the hood pulled low over his face. Fear runs through me.

"Hayden!" I hear Clive call out, and then his heavy footsteps can be heard running through the hall. "Are you okay?" I look over at Clive and I know he can see the panic in my face. My heart is literally beating out of my chest.

"I saw someone out there, standing beside the pond."

"Who? Was it Blade?" he asks, and nerves flutter though me. It wasn't Blade. It was too dark to actually tell who it was. For a minute there though...*I thought it was Michael.*

"No...he seemed bigger," I trail off lamely, ringing my hands together. Clive pulls me into his arms, leading me from the window—*which I guess isn't the smartest place to be at the moment.*

Clive helps me to sit on the edge of the bed and then he leans down on his knees in front of me. His hands rest on each of my arms. His blue eyes look into mine, filled with worry. He's a good man. Completely different from anyone I've ever met—for one he's completely at home wearing a suit. It's all I've seen him wear, to be honest. He's tall, but not a giant. Tall enough to where I feel feminine next to him but not scared. He's got eyes that are a bright, vibrant blue and kindness shimmers in them. His skin is dark, and his blondish-brown hair is cut short to his head in a style reminiscent of the military. He's completely opposite of any man I've ever met and nothing makes that clearer than the kindness he shows me. He handles me with care all the time. Even when I'm sure I probably drive him completely insane.

"I'm going to go outside and check it out. You take this and call 911 if I'm not back in ten minutes."

"But..." I start to argue, not wanting him to go outside in the rain. I'm sure I imagined it all. Michael was on my mind, and I somehow dreamed him up. *God knows I seem to do that every night.*

"No buts. I'm locking the door. If you hear the alarm go off because the correct code wasn't entered, you call 911 and then you call Victor."

"Clive I'm sure—"

"Hayden," he comes back at me in that warning tone he uses sometimes. I sigh, knowing any further argument is useless.

"I'll call."

"Good girl," he says. I huff out a large breath of air—annoyed with myself and Clive.

I watch him walk away. A second later, I hear the click of the front door. I look over at the window, feeling a little stupid. My hand goes down to my stomach, rubbing it gently.

"No one's out there, little one. Mommy just lost it for a minute. No one is coming after us," I tell her quietly. I feel a slight quiver against the palm of my hand, reassured. Maggie hasn't moved a lot in the last few days. The doctor assured me it's because she's getting ready for the birth, but I can't help but worry. "No one's coming for us," I tell her again, closing my eyes and trying to calm my nerves.

*No one is coming.* I repeat in my head. No one. *Especially not Michael.*

## ❦ 3 ❦

# BEAST

"Y ou're scaring her. What the fuck do you think you're doing, standing out in the wide open where she can see you?" Clive growls, rounding the corner of the house.

"Go back in, and leave me alone—*Clivey*," I respond, using the nickname that I've heard Hayden use once or twice.

"Not until you and I come to an understanding. Victor allows you to keep an eye on Hayden, but if I tell him you're terrifying her, he'll put a stop to it. You need to pack up and go back to that damned barn and leave Hayden alone. She doesn't need you in her life anymore—she never did."

"Worried she'll kick you to the curb, Stroker?" I ask him, stepping under the overhang of the house enough so that I can light a cigarette. I can't remember when I took up smoking. It was after Hayden left, when my nerves were shot, and I needed something to do with my hands. It's a nasty habit that I need to kick, but there's no point. There's no point in anything...

"I'm her bodyguard," his says, backing away from me.

"But we both know you want more. You can lie to yourself, but don't bother trying it with me."

"You'd be the last person Hayden would want in her life."

"Probably, but that was my choice. She wouldn't pick you, though, and that fact eats you up inside. I've seen how you stare after her, how you hang on her every word. Got a small tip for you Stroker. Women don't want a man they can lead around by the dick. You need to grow some balls."

"Bastard," he snarls and I have to laugh.

"Run back in the house, Clivey. Maybe you'll get lucky and she'll let you help her pick out what shoes to wear tomorrow," I sneer.

"You really are a miserable sack of shit," Stroker says, walking off.

He's right, I am. There's not a fucking thing I could say to that. I'm completely miserable. I miss Hayden so much I ache inside. I shouldn't, but I can't resist walking back around the side of the house. I stay deeper in the shadows this time, but I watch her bedroom window, hoping for just one more glimpse of her. I'm not sure how long it takes. Twenty? Maybe thirty minutes later, Hayden stands in front of the window again. She leans her head against it just like she does every night and she looks up at the sky.

The rain has begun to soak through the poncho and into my clothes. It has me chilled, but I can't really feel it. I'm always cold. It seems like I've been cold for a decade...if not, then at least since I've lost Annabelle. I drop my cigarette to the ground, letting the rain extinguish it. I wonder—just like I always do, exactly what Hayden has on her mind when she stares up at the sky. Is she thinking about Maggie? The future? *Me?* I curse this need clawing inside of me to claim her. It's too late. It always was...just too late.

"My turn yet, Sunshine?" My head jerks as Devil comes around the corner. I shake my head. I really don't know why I like this bastard, yet I do. I have even less of an idea why I agreed to let him come to Wyoming with me.

"I'm good. You can have the night off."

"You sure? You look like you could use some sleep. Actually, you look like you could use a hell of a lot more, but you should start with sleep."

"Whatever. Don't you have some woman you can go play with?"

"Always, amigo," he smirks.

"You've been hanging around Skull too much."

"I've had to do some business there for Diesel. Skull's not a bad guy. Gets a little touchy when I hug Beth goodbye," he cracks and I just shake my head. If he's hugged Beth, it's a wonder he still has hands.

"I'm staying here. You can come by in the morning."

"You know chances are she'd be fine without us watching."

"Aren't you the fucker who encouraged me to come after her?" I ask him, my eyes going back to Hayden, who has stopped looking at the sky and is now looking out over the lawn. I want to walk towards her. Let her see me. *I don't.*

"Absolutely. Still, I meant, go claim your woman. Bend her over a desk, give her a good fuck and stop being an idiot. *That* clearly didn't happen," he half laughs. I flip him off and he laughs harder.

"I told you if you're tired, you can go home. I'm fine on my own. *I prefer it.*"

"There you go spreading joy and happiness again. I'm good, asshole. I just think you need to claim your woman, before you lose her."

"She's not mine. I just want to make sure her and the baby are safe until Blade is caught."

"What if he's never caught? Fuck, he's probably given up on her and is sunning it up on some beach in Mexico, living the good life."

"He's out there somewhere," I tell Devil, and I'm sure of it. I've never been surer of anything in my life.

"What makes you say that?"

"Because he's a moron."

"Well I can't argue with that, but still—"

"And Hayden is not the kind of girl a man just walks away from. Not even a twisted, sick fuck like Blade." Devil watches me for a minute. It feels like he's dissecting me. He shrugs and for once he doesn't come back with some asinine retort.

"I'll see you in the morning, Sunshine. I'll bring doughnuts," he says, walking off. I grunt in reply, watching his back disappear around the house. "And coffee. Lots of coffee," he adds and I'm definitely okay with that. Wish I had some now.

I turn my attention away from him and back to Hayden. She's no longer standing in front of the window now and there's immediate disappointment. I slide down to the ground, ignoring the wetness. I look up at the sky and thunder roars above me and the rain increases.

*It's going to be a long night.*

## ❧ 4 ❧

## HAYDEN

"**A**re you okay, Hayden?" D.D. asks me. I look up from the cupcakes I'm frosting to respond and have to laugh. D.D. is one of the three girls that I have working for me, but out of them all D.D. is the one I trust the most. I quickly made her manager of the bakery and she keeps me from going insane. Her name is actually Dessurè, but it's not pronounced at all like it sounds, so I call her D.D.—or pain in my ass—depending on the day.

She's about my age—a little older. She has this red hair that is almost orange in color and she wears it short, having it end on the back of her neck. She's covered in freckles, has kind brown eyes, and a smile that always makes you want to return it. Right now, she's not smiling. She's frowning—her face full of concern for me. Which means I've not been hiding things as well as I thought I had. I sigh, putting down the tube of delicate buttercream icing I was piping.

"You worry too much," I chastise.

"That's not an answer, woman," she comes back at me. I back up to the seat I'm standing by and sit down thankfully. We're in the kitchen of my bakery. D.D. and I are working in here today and I've got Jenn out front.

"Why are you asking?"

"Maybe because you're putting the vanilla buttercream on the Henderson cupcakes, when they're supposed to have the lavender white chocolate frosting."

"Shit..."

"And you put it on wrong, even after I corrected you twice," she adds. I look at the twenty cupcakes I've already completed from the order of fifty and I want to cry. It was a special order for caramel cupcakes which means I'll have to do another batch to make up for the twenty that are now wrong. It also means I'll have to make another batch of the vanilla buttercream because that was for another order.

"Shit, shit, shit!" I mutter, disgusted with myself.

"Yeah. So, why don't you tell me what's going on?"

"It's nothing, honest. I just...didn't sleep well last night and I'm paying for it today."

"You never sleep. Are you still thinking about...*him*?" she asks, and I almost regret telling her about Michael. Still, in the four weeks that I've known D.D. we've become really close. It's helped talking to her too. Heck, I talk to her almost as much as the therapist that Victor set me up with.

"I saw him last night," I confess sadly, rubbing my lower back because it hurts like hell today. I still have a bit to go before Maggie makes an appearance, but I swear at this rate when she does get here, I'm going to throw a party.

"You saw him?" she screeches. "*He's in Wyoming?!?!*"

"Yes...no—at least I don't think so."

"Well that makes perfect sense," she laughs.

"I was sure he was out there. I didn't see a face, but everything else reminded me of him. I really thought it was, but Clive went outside and said no one was there. Which means it was probably just my mind playing tricks on me."

"You need to forget that man," D.D. advises for like the

millionth time. She's right of course. The only problem, is that... I'm starting to think that's impossible.

"D.D. —"

"Besides girl, you have a Grade-A, prime specimen living in the same house with you. You need to quit daydreaming over some jack-off that doesn't deserve your time, jump on the Clive train, and ride him all the way home."

"Will you stop? I've told you a hundred times that Clive and I don't have that type of relationship. Besides, I'm as big as the side of a house. Even if I felt like having sex these days—which I don't —I doubt Clive would even look twice at me."

"Please girl! That man eats you alive with his eyes. And hey, sex might be just what the doctor orders."

"What are you talking about now?" I ask her, ignoring her remark about Clive. I can't think about that. Surely she's wrong. I like Clive, but...I don't think of him that way. I don't want him to think of me like that. If he did...*that's just too complicated.*

"Sex, of course. Here take your ruined cupcakes out and have Jenn put them in the display case. Maybe they will sell to the lunch crowd. I'll bring these peanut butter kisses out," she says, changing the subject.

I look at the clock. It's almost noon and she's right. There's a good chance they will sell if we get them out. With a groan, I slide out of my seat and grab the tray of cupcakes, walking behind her. Sometimes I wonder who's the boss—her or me. I'm pretty sure it's her.

"I know you're talking about sex and I already told you, that's the last thing that's on my mind. Besides, as big as I am, it would be the last thing on any man's mind. Especially since it's not his baby. I don't know what world you are living in, but pregnant women aren't exactly high on a man's *must have* list." I sigh.

The bakery is empty. Hopefully the lunch hour brings a rush of customers. I'm doing good on custom orders, but day to day business has been hit or miss—and there's a lot more missing than hitting. Victor assured me it just takes time, he's even offered to pay the mortgage payment for me, but it's important to me that I do this on my own. I need to prove it to myself, as well as everyone else, that I can stand on my own two feet. My mantra used to be that I'd be stronger. Now? I don't have a mantra. I am strong. I survived losing Michael. If I can do that, I can do anything.

"Please, woman. We both know men are always sniffing around you. It's like you have pheromones that smell like bacon."

"Pheromones?" I laugh, putting the cupcakes in the front display case. Jenn automatically begins helping me.

"Yeah, those things we women release that make men want to push us against the wall and slam us into next week? Well, most women anyways. I release them and they say: *Yay time to fuck D.D. over again. Maybe we'll kick her dog too, when we're done.*"

"Oh, stop."

"I'm just saying. If I had a Clive in my life, I'd strip him naked and ask him how he wanted me."

"You would not!" I chastise her.

"Honey, I would in a heartbeat," she responds back.

"Is Clive that hot dude in the suit who follows you around like a little lost puppy?" Jenn asks.

"He does not," I immediately argue, feeling my face heat with embarrassment.

"He does," D.D. argues—she seems to be really argumentative today.

"I miss him. The day went faster when we could look at his sexy ass. How come he stopped hanging out here?"

"We got the security system put in. I demanded Clive at least take time off while I'm at the store."

"Then I think I hate you, Hayden. I miss Clive. I kind of want him to shave his head bald. He'd look hot bald."

"You think all bald men are sexy and I got to tell you, Jenn, they are *not*," D.D. says emphatically. "Most of the time their heads look like giant penises!"

"Hey! I like penises," Jenn says, and I can't help but laugh. I love these girls.

"So do I, but not on their flipping heads," D.D. responds, laughing.

"Hey," she shrugs, "I'd climb up on the counter and straddle his head. I'm game."

"Oh my shit," D.D. cries, laughing. I can't help but join in, at the picture of Jenn straddling Clive's head.

"You two need to stop. Besides, I think Clive is gay."

"Get out of town. For real?" Jenn whines. "I just hate that."

"What?" I ask, not understanding Jenn's problem.

"Why men that look as fine as Clive have to crave the D. I mean I know why I crave the D, but there's such a shortage of good, sexy man-meat. I hate having to give up a candidate."

"I don't think he's gay. I don't get that at all, and my gay-dar is usually spot on. Besides he looks at you like he wants to eat you alive. And by eat I'm talking with his mouth—not a fork," D.D. interjects.

"God, it's been so long since I've been ate—" Jenn stops as the bell to the door goes off, signaling a customer.

"I hate both of you and your sex talk," I mutter, ignoring the bell—because as the owner I can do that.

"Fuck!" D.D. growls, and most of the time she says anything but fuck, so I'm immediately alarmed. I look up to see a young teen standing at the door. He looks like he weighs ninety pounds soaking wet. He's pale and has dyed his hair a deep black that falls just on his shoulders. He looks like he might be sixteen, possibly a little older, but not a lot. That's not what is alarming though. What's alarming is the gun he's holding in his shaking hands and aiming at Jenn.

"Hand over your money," he orders.

*Crap.*

## ❧ 5 ❧

# BEAST

"How much is that pussy in the window. The one with the waggly tail...." Devil sings and I slap him on the back of the head. "Hey! What the hell was that for?"

"Stop looking at my...at Hayden," I grunt. We're at an outside café across the street from Hayden's bakery. Again I find myself looking through a window like a damned peeping Tom, just to get a glimpse of her. Devil just showed up to relieve me so I could go get some rest, but even after not sleeping all night—I couldn't leave. I don't sleep much anyways. So here I am with my ass parked in a hard, metal chair, staring through a window. It's a good view. Hayden's place has these large, open-area windows. So open that when she came in with a tray of cupcakes, I could see her clearly. My damn heart sped up, pumping so hard it hurt. I rub the area in reflex.

"I'm talking about that hot mama standing beside her. The one with the chestnut colored hair and big tits, and damn that ass. I'd like to bend that over and ride it hard."

"Chestnut?"

"Yeah, man. The kind that drags down your chest, wraps around your cock, while she's sucking your nuts."

"Jesus you're a freak."

"Never claimed to be different. Fuck me though, I need to hit that."

I'm tuning Devil out, it's not easy, because he never shuts up. I'm busy staring at Hayden. I'm dying to touch her, to kiss her... Hell, even just talking to her would be good. It's not happening. This is useless. I need to fucking crash before I do something stupid like give in and go to her. I grunt, I don't know if it's at the way Devil's going on about the woman in the bakery—because he's still talking about her, or if it's because I'm on the verge of going in and throwing Hayden over my shoulder.

"I'm heading home," I mutter. Home is a joke. It's a seedy motel on the edge of this hole-in-the-wall town. The mattress feels like rocks and the smell reminds me of an old gym. I sigh, my back hurts getting up from the chair. I'm too old for this shit. I'm too old to be mooning over a woman and a life I can't have. Maybe I should just stop. Trust Victor and Clive to take care of Hayden. She's not mine, not anymore.

"Okay, Sunshine. Get that beauty rest. You sure as fuck need it," Devil cracks.

I take a few steps away, throwing up my middle finger at him—which only makes the asshole laugh. It's then I feel it. A chill that moves through my entire body. It makes the hairs on the back of my neck stand at attention. If that wasn't enough to warn me something was happening, I could have sworn I heard a soft voice whisper one small word in my ear. *"Stay."*

"You okay, man?" Devil asks and out of the corner of my eye I see him stand. That nervous feeling intensifies, flying through me, and setting me on edge. My time in the military taught me to trust my gut instincts, but this is different. This is more intense. I scan the area, almost positive that Blade is in the area. He's the only enemy on my mind. The streets seem calm and clear though. I'm about to shrug it off. Not sleeping is obviously fucking with me, that has to be it. Just to reassure myself I take one last look at Hayden. She's standing up now, the pan of cupcakes having been transferred into a cabinet. Even from this distance though, something seems off about her. She seems tense. She's talking to a customer and my eyes take him in. It's a tall, skinny figure with jet black hair. He's wearing a thick hoodie and gloves. That's strange in and of itself, because it's like eighty fucking degrees out here. Then I see it. A flash of metal as the sun shines through the window, reflecting on it. The man's holding a gun. *He's holding a gun on Hayden.*

I take off running towards the store, Devil just a step or two behind me. I've got to save her. *I have to.*

## ❧ 6 ❧

# HAYDEN

"Listen asshole," Jenn starts. I love Jenn. She's a take-no-shit kind of girl. She tells you straight out if she does or doesn't like something, you're not left guessing. Jenn loves with her whole heart, but she also has no filter. She says the first thing that hits her—like now. Which I'm more than fine with, but right now with the man pointing a gun at her—at all of us, I'd wish she would rein it in.

"Do as he says, Jenn," I whisper, doing my best to remain calm. If I needed a sign to prove that I am stronger, I have it. Because I'm not in the middle of a panic attack. Still, I am scared. My hand goes to my stomach and I do my best to remain behind the display case. It's not really protection for Maggie, but it's the best I can manage at the moment. I look out the corner of my eye at D.D. and she nods carefully. Instantly I know that she has triggered the silent alarm. Fingers crossed they get here soon, or this guy gets what he wants and leaves.

"You the one in charge here?" the man asks and I ignore the sinking feeling in my stomach. The one that says I shouldn't have attracted the attention of the crazy man.

"I am," I tell him, proud of how calm my voice is.

"How about you take me in the back and show me where you keep the safe," he says waving his gun like he's pointing it to the back room.

Revulsion and fear collide in my stomach, causing it to roll. I feel a fine, cold sweat pop out over me. I see the wild look in his eyes and I'm scared for my daughter. My hand goes to my stomach in reflex. If I was ever going to have another panic attack, it would be right now. The strangest thing happens, though. I feel this heat move through my body. I don't know how to explain it, it's a warmth, a sweetness and in the air there's a scent of strawberries. Then I hear a soft voice. It's distant and I know it's not anyone around me. Yet, I hear it all the same.

*"It's okay,"* a soft, feminine voice whispers. *"It's okay."*

I'm losing my mind. It's finally happened. It was bound to happen, really. I mean, with everything I've endured and now this, who could remain sane? Obviously not me.

"I said the back room, lady. *Now,*" the man orders, demanding my attention again.

"We don't have a safe," D.D. answers for me.

"Was I talking to you, bitch?" the man growls and he takes aim at D.D. I can't let her get shot. I just can't.

"She's right!" I tell him in a panicked voice. "I've not been open that long. We haven't had enough business to warrant getting one."

"You're lying!" he growls, anger making his pale face, blotch red in places.

"Look around, Einstein. How many customers do you see?" Jenn scoffs, love her heart. If we survive this, I may hug her to death—*or choke her.*

"You bitch," the man snarls, and the gun he's holding moves back so it's pointing at Jenn.

The rest is kind of a blur, because in that next moment the bell on the door rings. "Get out!" I yell, without looking because the last thing we need is more people in here getting hurt. I take the pan I'm holding and throw it at the man as he takes aim at Jenn.

"Get the fuck down!" I hear this big burly growl. I want to look towards it, but I can't. The gun goes off and I go down behind the counter. There's a rush of movement in front of me as someone literally leaps from the front door to the counter and tackles Jenn, bringing her down on the ground. I wince as they hit the floor, but luckily he twists in the air and lands so that he takes the brunt of their fall. That's going to leave a bruise. *Devil.* I thought I was panicked before, but now...I stand and *I see him.*

Michael has tackled the man with the gun to the floor. He's taken it away from him. I wince when he takes the butt of the gun and hits the side of the boy's head. Michael stands up and the roar of anger he lets out, can probably be heard two counties over. He pulls his leg back and delivers a strong kick to the other man's mid-section.

"Michael," I gasp, unable to believe he's here.

"You motherfucking piece of shit!" he's yelling and delivering kick after kick. "Get up and fight me like a fucking man, you pussy," he demands and the anger that's coming from him is so huge, so *intense* that it stifles the air in the room.

"Oh, my shit," D.D. murmurs, coming to stand beside me. She puts her hand on my arm and I absently pat it, but my attention is on Michael.

"I don't think he can fight you, Sunshine. I'm pretty sure the fucker is unconscious and if you kick him with that steel-toed boot again, his ribs are probably going to be ground to dust," Devil says. I can see him standing and helping Jenn to stand at the same time, his arm protectively around her.

"Michael, stop," I order him, when I manage to find my voice again and make it stronger. He looks up at me and the fury and emotion swirling in his eyes could make me dizzy. He does stop kicking the man, however.

"Oh fuck. *This* is Michael?" I hear D.D. in the background. I don't look at her. I'm staring at the man who has haunted me for the past two months. The man who has let his hair grow back out, *again*. The man who is wearing his rage like a second skin, and finally the man who is staring at me like an animal—a beast, getting ready to devour me.

Yeah.

*This is Michael.*

# 7

# BEAST

I slowly calm down. The anger I felt when I saw the gun is unlike anything I can describe. I'm barely containing it— even now. I want to pull the motherfucker up by his throat and choke the life out of him. I might have, if the police hadn't chosen that moment to pull up. They slowly take over, asking the girls and me questions. I don't answer, luckily Devil jumps in for me. I've barely taken my eyes off Hayden. She's talking to the cops, but I see her look up at me, warily, every so often. I wish I knew what was going through her head. I wish I knew what to say to her.

Eventually everyone is cleared out with the exception of the girls, Devil and me. There's a strained silence and Hayden and I are just staring at each other. I find myself rubbing along the side of my face, finding the largest scar and touching it, needing something to ground me.

"Well that was exciting. What's your name, sweet thing?" Devil asks, breaking the silence. I look over at him and see he's putting his moves on the girl he tackled to the floor.

"Jenn. Jenn Allen," she says, and there's the faintest color of red creeping up on her face. She's flustered at his attention, but you'd have to be stupid not to see the spark of interest shining in her eyes.

"Well hey there Jenn Allen, they call me Devil."

"Devil?" she asks, with a confused, nervous laugh.

"That's right baby. Think you'd like to sin with me?" he laughs. If my eyes weren't glued on Hayden, I'd be slapping him upside the head right now. I hear giggling and then he and Jenn walk into the other room. Hayden and I still don't speak. Her other friend stands there for a minute. The air between all of us is awkward. I have a feeling that's not getting better any time soon.

"Are you okay, Hay?" her friend asks. I can hear the protective note in her voice. It grates on my nerves—*even if I understand it.*

I watch as Hayden clears her throat. Then she tears her eyes away from me. "I'm fine, D.D. Can you give me a few minutes alone with Michael?"

"Are you sure?"

"Yeah. I'll be fine," she answers, but her face doesn't look like she believes it. Hell, I'm not that sure I'll be fine. I never planned on letting her know I was here. I wouldn't have if there had been any other way. Hayden takes her hand and rubs her lower back. She's done it a few times, even during the hold up. She's overdoing it, and I know these concrete floors are too much for her. She should be at home with her feet up. Why Victor ever thought this bakery was a good idea is beyond me. He should have convinced her to stay home and relax until after the baby arrives.

"I guess I can go see what Jenn and uh.... the Devil are up to, then," she mutters. I could tell her what they are probably doing, but I want her gone. I want her gone and yet at the same time I want her to stay. If she's here, Hayden won't talk about our past. If she's here, I can just stare at Hayden a little longer before I leave. I rub that spot under my beard that I always do when I begin to feel anxious. I can't take my eyes off of Hayden, even if I tried. I hear her friend's shoes click against the concrete floors, but Hayden's eyes are back on me and that requires all of my attention. A door squeaks and then her friend speaks again. "I'll just be in the next room. If you need me, just call out," she says. I grunt my displeasure, that woman is getting on my nerves.

"I'll be fine," Hayden replies. A few moments later I hear the door slam shut. It does nothing to help the tension in the room dissipate. It might actually increase. We stare at each other a little longer. It's almost a standoff. Finally, Hayden lowers her face, rubbing the tension at the bridge of her nose. When she looks back up at me I can see pain there and I hate that I caused it. "Why are you here, Michael?"

"You need protection," I respond, feeling so uncomfortable my skin tingles, the burns and nerve endings on my legs are even more annoying than normal.

"I didn't mean now. Though I guess I should be thankful you came along at the exact right moment."

"I didn't," I interrupt her, meaning I've been here all along, but I'm not telling her that.

"That's okay I'm not thankful either," she says and if I rub my beard any harder, I'll rub the damn thing off. "It was you outside my home last night, wasn't it?" she asks and maybe I should deny it —but, I don't. I grunt in reply. For a second there's a ghost of a smile on her face and then her beautiful gray eyes cloud with pain and the smile is gone. "Why were you there?" she asks, her voice quieter.

"Protecting you," I answer again. Her face is covered with shock and then confusion. I can almost see the way her brain is sorting through the facts and how she arrives at her answer. I'm pretty sure she comes up with the right one when anger becomes the strongest emotion I get from her.

"I've been gone for two months, Michael. Is there some reason you felt the urge to track me down in Wyoming this week and begin *protecting* me, or do I have a full moon or something to curse as the reason?" she sighs coming from behind the counter. Hayden doesn't get close to me, but she sits down not far from me. She looks tired. She puts her hands on top of the table, wringing them together in that nervous action she always had. My hand literally shakes with the need to wrap it around one of hers. Of all the things I've missed, the strongest of all of those might be just holding her hand. Ain't that just another bucket of fuck? *Christ*. I don't even know who I am anymore. "Michael?" she prompts and I growl, giving up rubbing the scar under my beard. Nothing is making this easier, none of this is calming me.

"I've been here since you moved out here, Hayden."

I watch as her eyes dilate with that news as the truth sinks in. I expected screaming and yelling, but I forgot that somehow Hayden always surprises me. "Why?" she asks quietly.

This time it's me who clears their throat and it has nothing to do with my injuries. *This time it's all nerves.* "I made a promise to protect you and Maggie and that's what I'm going to do."

"You made a promise...So Maggie and I are a responsibility to you?"

"A promise, and one I intend to keep."

"Then I release you of that responsibility. Maggie and I don't need you. We don't want you in our lives anymore," she responds and I'd be a motherfucking liar if I didn't admit that cut me straight through. My chest hurts so bad I flinch.

"It doesn't work that way. I'm here until Blade is found."

"That's ridiculous!" she cries, standing up agitated. "I have protection. Victor makes sure of that and I have Clive! I'm perfectly safe!"

"Today would argue that," I mutter, feeling anger peek through the millions of other emotions Hayden makes me feel.

"You need to leave, Michael. I'll ask Clive to start staying at the store. I'll be fine. *You* need to go," she orders. She's standing now. She walks to the door, as if to point the way. I hate that she keeps bringing up Stroker. It's like she's waving a red flag at a bull—*me being the bull*. I'm sick of it.

"I'm here and I'm not going anywhere. Stroker or no Stroker," I inform her. As I say the words, I walk over and stare her down. My words are a deep throaty growl, meant to intimidate. Hayden doesn't even blink. She brings her hand back and slaps me across the face. It's a good hit, one that connects and sends heat instantly through me. I grab her wrist not letting her take her hand away.

"Get out," she cries, though her voice is quieter. Anger has made her face flush red and her eyes have tears gathered in them that stubbornly refuse to fall.

"No," I tell her, moving my hand from her wrist and wrapping it around her palm and fingers, almost forcing her to hold my hand —even though our fingers don't interlock. I don't care. It's still the closest I've felt to being alive in months.

*I'm not going anywhere.*

## 8

# HAYDEN

"I hate you!" I cry, trying to jerk my hand away, but he doesn't let me. His touch is agony—searing me with heat and a need I've been trying to forget for two months. I hate him. *God.* I hate him so much. I hate him for making me love him. I hate him for pushing me away. I hate him for destroying me with his words. I hate him for leaving me alone for two months. But, most of all, *I hate him for coming back.* Coming back, not because he cared, or because he missed me too. He came back to catch Blade. He views me and Maggie as a responsibility.

*He came back to leave again.*

I drag air through my lungs. They feel raw, just like the rest of me right now.

"I hate myself," he answers and for a moment he looks so lost... so broken that some of my anger fades.

I had Victor collect information on Michael that first month. I read about his daughter, his club and exactly what my brother did to destroy them. I learned Michael's wife was a self-centered bitch who used their daughter against him. I learned the hell Michael's life had been before he found the club and then after. I always knew he was broken. I never realized how deep it went. The one thing that stood out above everything else—and there was a lot. The one thing—was looking at a picture of Annabelle. She was beautiful. Long blonde hair with ringlet curls and a heart-shaped face that accentuated her chubby cheeks so well you wish you could touch them...*kiss them*. Her eyes though, were like round sparkly blue diamonds with enough warmth in them to fill the world. She was special. Everything about her picture told you that and reading how she died, how men had to drag Michael away from the burning carnage destroyed me. This man. This beautifully scarred, broken man—who so easily crushed me, was damaged in ways I would never understand. He was shattered into a million fragments inside and all of them were jagged and rough. All of them would leave you bleeding if you touched them. It would be suicide to soften towards him again. It would be suicide to try and hold him.

"Don't do this, Michael. I'm not strong enough to withstand you again," I plead.

"I'm sorry, Beauty." The nickname is like a knife going through my heart. Plunging in so painfully that I can't help but gasp from the pain and shock.

"Don't. Don't call me that again," I whisper, agony laced in my voice so thick it makes it hoarse. "Never again," I tell him, my eyes closing and the tears I had been restraining break free and I hate that I feel them on my cheeks. I hate that I can't control them.

*I hate that I still love him.*

I keep my eyes shut as Michael brings his hand up. I feel his fingers barely touch the side of my face, touching along my jawline and under my eyes. His thumb brushes against the tears and I hear his breathing. It seems so loud that all other sounds in the room stop. Everything seems to stop existing except me and Michael.

"I'm sorry, Beauty," he whispers in his deep, gruff voice that I remember so well—ignoring my plea. My body trembles from the force of holding back my sobs.

"You pushed me away. You're already planning on leaving again. Why couldn't you just stay away, Michael? I needed you to stay away," I tell him, eyes still closed. The last sentence I say in a broken whisper that you can barely hear. At least I can't hear it. It's drowned out by the way my heart is beating in my chest and the fear rushing through my blood.

"I can't. God help me, Hayden. *I can't,*" he says, and I cry harder.

"What's going on in here?" I hear Clive asking as the bell on the door goes off, announcing his entry.

I don't answer him. I can't right now. Truthfully, I wish he hadn't showed up. Michael pulls me into his arms and I should be stronger. *I really should be.* But, I go willingly. I fall against him and it feels like I'm breathing for the first time in months. I take in his scent, how safe I feel in this moment and I relax against him, letting his chest catch my tears. His arm goes around me—just one. With the other, he changes his hold on my hand and our fingers wrap around one another, linking. Holding hands just like we always did. *Just like the past two months never happened.*

But they did...

## ❧ 9 ❧

## BEAST

It's like my heart has started beating again for the first time in months. That's exactly how it feels when Hayden's fingers wrap around mine and she falls into my body. *Life where there once was death.* I don't know what I expected when I saw her again, but the fact that she's in my arms is all I care about. I hate that she's crying. I hate that the pain coming off of her in waves has only one reason—me. Yet, even with all of that all I can feel is relief. I don't deserve this. I know I don't. There is so much pain in her eyes. It seems wrong that her pain brings the first moment of peace I've had in a long time. Hayden is back in my arms. *I can breathe again.*

"What's going on in here?" Clive growls, but I don't let it stop me. I continue pulling Hayden as close to me as I can, drinking her in. Everything. Her touch, her feel, her scent and her breath, they all belong to me in this moment and it's like a needle in the vein to an addict going through detox.

"Took you awhile to get here, Stroker." I answer. I don't let go of Hayden, even when she tries to pull away. I do allow her to turn —in my arms. I purposely use his last name, because he hates it. Can't say I blame him. I just wish that his first name made it a little more interesting. *Dick.* His parents should have named him Dick.

"I wrongly thought you and your buddy were watching Hayden. You okay, sweetheart?" he asks, and I could cheerfully punch him in his face right now. *Sweetheart? Fuck no.*

"I'm...wait...*you knew Michael was in town?*" Hayden asks and I find myself grinning. Clive gives me a fuck-off look, which makes my smile broaden.

"Hayden, Victor allowed it, there wasn't much I could do—."

"You should have told me, Clive. You shouldn't have kept this from me. You've been lying to me," she responds. *"What is it with me?* Why do I keep attracting men I can't trust?" she whispers, and that wipes the smile from my face.

"Hayden," I start, and Clive does at the same time. We both look at each other at the same time and if hate were a physical thing, you'd definitely felt its presence right now.

"I don't want to hear it. From either of you," she warns, and she pulls from my hold again. I let her go, but I instantly miss her hand in mine.

"D.D.!" she yells out, rubbing her forehead above her eye.

"Hayden—" Clive begins, but she holds her hand out—shutting him down.

"Not now. Maybe not ever. Isn't this supposed to be your time off? You can go. As you can see I have one too many bodyguards now," she huffs motioning to me, and just like that the grin comes back.

"We need to talk," Clive answers.

"We can talk tonight at home. I can't deal with it right now, Clive. I honestly can't."

"I'll make tacos for dinner," he tells her and just like that the grin is gone again. I need this fucker gone. Victor's going to have to call him off, or I'll kill him. The choices are clear.

"Fine. I won't need you to pick me up here though. I'll have D.D. drop me off," she sighs.

"No," we both say at the same time. I snarl at Clive. There's only so much a fucking man can take. "I'll drop you off," I growl. *I don't add that I'm going in, and I'm not leaving.* I hate that she used the word home with Clive. *I want to kill him.*

"Whatever," she sighs. "D.D.!" she growls out and to be completely honest her growl might be better than mine. Clive leaves quietly, making sure to shoot me yet another look of dislike. The feeling is more than mutual and I will be talking to Victor about it. Hayden and I are stuck looking at each other, both of us with a lot to say, but neither one of us wanting to approach it.

D.D. comes out of the back room, fixing her hair and adjusting her shirt. Her lipstick is smeared. Behind her Devil and Jenn come out and Jenn is in much the same shape. Devil is grinning like the fucking asshole he always is.

"Um. What's up?" D.D. asks, still trying to fix her hair.

"Oh my God. You didn't. *Both of you?*" Hayden cries. Devil leans back against the counter, looking extremely happy with himself. *Fuck.* Or maybe that's just the look when you get your dick somewhere you really want it. I look over at Hayden. It's been so long I can't remember.

"I don't want to talk about it," D.D. mutters, blushing.

"Don't be so shocked Hayden, it's just three people enjoying themselves. I'd be game to show you exactly how fun sinning can be," he winks. "But I'd rather not piss Sunshine off. I'm partial to my dick," Devil jokes and I grunt, wondering how long it'd take to suffocate him with my hands around his neck.

"D.D. I need you to run me down to the police station to file a report."

"No you don't. I'm taking you."

"What? Of course you aren't. D.D. will take me," Hayden argues.

"You need to reopen the store for business. So she needs to be here. I'll take you. Besides we need to talk."

"I think we've said entirely too much to each other."

"Probably, but there's still things to say. Are you ready to leave now?"

"Fine, but you take me downtown and then home and that's it. We part ways and we never have to see each other again."

"Let's go Beauty," I answer, ignoring what she said. I put my hand on her back and begin directing her toward the door.

"I asked you not to call me that," she whispers. I grunt in reply.

"Hey Sunshine, I'll just stick around here and keep an eye on the ladies," Devil says, and I close the door on him.

I really have no idea why I like the bastard.

## 10

## BEAST

"I thought you were leaving?" Hayden mutters when I make it evident I'm coming inside her house. I do this by pushing through the door when she unlocks it—after first grunting when she refused to give me her house keys.

"You thought wrong," I mumble, scratching my beard. "Where's Stroker?"

"What are you doing here?"

"Get used to it," I grumble at Stroker's question. "In fact, you can have the night off."

"I can?"

"He can?" Hayden mimics.

"Yeah, cause I'm here tonight instead of outside. I'll make sure Hayden's safe."

"The hell you are," Stroker answers.

"No, you're not," Hayden argues. I growl, rubbing the back of my neck. Everything has to be a fight with this woman.

"You were shot at today," I remind her.

"I was not shot at. A gun was drawn and it was directed at Jenn and—"

"Whatever! You could have been killed. Maggie could have

been killed. I promised to protect *both* of you and that's exactly what I'm doing."

"Just how do you plan on doing that?" she asks, hands on her hips and her cheeks flushed. With her stomach sticking out like it does now, she looks beautiful, just like this. I rub my chest, getting that strange feeling yet again, one of heat and pain.

"I'm moving in."

"Fuck no," Stroker growls. He's getting on my nerves. I toss him my cell. He catches it as it bounces off his stomach.

"Call your boss," I smirk. He glares at me and leaves the room, hopefully to go call Victor.

"Michael—"

"Do you want me to leave, Hayden?" I ask her deciding to cut through all the bullshit.

"Yes! I do!"

"You're lying."

"I—"

"Before you answer that, I know you're angry."

"I am," she says, shock on her face.

"I know you're..."

"Hurt? You hurt me, Michael. Worse than anyone ever has because I *cared* about you."

"I know you probably won't believe me, Hayden, but I care about you too."

I watch as she brings her tongue out to moisten her bottom lip, and then she bites it. She's not doing it to be sexy, though it is. She's nervous. *She's scared.* I wonder what she would think if she knew I was just as scared?

"You have a funny way of showing it."

"I'm fucked up Hayden. There's no other way to put it. I'm...I have a lot that I don't deal well with," I finish lamely, amazed at how pitiful that sums up the war inside of me.

"Annabelle," she says, whispering my daughter's name. It's like a kick in the gut, more painful than any physical blow.

"Yeah," I agree, my voice so thick it barely comes out.

"I saw a picture of her. She was beautiful, Michael."

"You did? How?"

"I asked Victor to get some information about you. I know it was wrong, but I... I wanted to understand, I wanted to..."

"It's okay, Hayden. I don't mind you knowing."

"I wish you had been the one to tell me. You should have told me, Michael. Before that night, I mean," she sighs, her hands clenching each other in that movement she always does when she's nervous or upset. I can't resist walking to her, and when I do I put my hand over both of hers.

"I'm sorry, Beauty. About that night, I was...I was hurting and raw inside. I just lashed out at you. I shouldn't have, you didn't deserve it. The things I said, about your brother..." I trail off, because there's not much I can really say here. I can't take them back, because they were said. I can't tell her they were lies, because they're not.

"Can we...I don't want to talk about my brother. I don't think I can. Not with you, at least not right now. I get what he cost you and your club. I know what he did to me. He wasn't a good person. But...I just can't deal with all that right now."

"Fair enough," I tell her clearing my throat.

"I don't want to leave, Hayden. I want...*I need* to stay here and protect you and Maggie. I need to know that you two are okay."

"And then you'll walk away? Leave us once you know we're safe?"

"I..."

"How will you even know if we are safe, Michael? Are you listening to yourself? You want to protect us from Blade and we don't even know if Blade is still out there. Life happens, Michael. Like today at the bakery. You can't prepare for everything. There's just no way. So whether you leave right now, or a week, even months down the road, there's just no way of knowing if we're safe. You're being unreasonable. It would be better if you just walk away now, before—"

"Before what, Hayden?"

"Before you make me care about you again," she says as if she's admitting a horrible secret, and maybe she is. But her words fire a hope inside of me I thought was dead and gone. I thought after that night, there was no way that Hayden could forgive me. I thought I lost the chance to ever touch her again. To just hear her laugh again would be a miracle for me.

"Then what if I don't leave?" I ask her, point blank wondering if she realizes how hard this is for me. Wondering if it's even harder on her.

"Don't...What are you saying, Michael?"

"When we made love, I claimed Maggie. You let me, Hayden. What if I don't leave."

"I can't...I'm tired Michael. I can't process this tonight. I need time...*to think*."

"Then take the time, but I'm staying here regardless. Tonight and every night following—"

"I just said I wasn't sure! I need time—"

"For now we'll say until Blade is tracked down or caught. Anything else...we'll take it one day at a time."

"Michael, we don't need to do this. I've been fine for two months. I have protection, I'm being watched over. Maggie and I are safe."

"I'm not leaving, Hayden. If I have to sit outside in the rain like last night, every night from here on—I will. I'm not leaving."

"You're not being reasonable."

"I know."

"I should have Victor escort you out of town and not even bother talking to you."

"I know that too."

"You're an asshole."

"I know—"

"Oh stop agreeing with me already. I'm trying to fight here. Fine! You can stay at least tonight. One false move and you're out, Michael."

"Duly noted, Beauty."

"There are rules," she grumbles and I have to fight to keep from smiling, because I'm pretty sure smiling right now would get me kicked in the balls.

"I'm listening," I assure her, already feeling like I won a war.

"You do not call me that nickname ever again."

"Hayden—"

"That's non-negotiable, Michael.

"I'll agree—for now," I warn her, not sure I can give her that. Her response is a growl under her breath.

"And I'm not able to, but I still want it stated, there will be no sleeping together."

"Done."

"You agreed to that awful quick," she mutters clearly put out. Again, it's all I can do to keep from grinning.

"I guess there's only one more question," I tell her, studying her face.

"What's that?" she asks, eyeing me warily.

"Are you going to tell Clive? Or am I?" I ask, and I do grin this time.

"You really are an asshole," she mutters with a sigh and I resist the urge to lean into her and kiss her forehead.

## ❦ II ❦

# HAYDEN

My house is way too quiet. There's no possible way you can sleep in all this screaming...*silence*. I can't help being scared about letting Michael stay. It was stupid, but the truth is, I don't want him to leave. If I'm being entirely honest, I'm hoping that I can keep him this time. How pathetic is that? It's the truth though. I can admit it—at least to myself. I rub my stomach gently.

"Mommy is hopeless, baby girl," I whisper. Maggie pushes against my hand in response—probably in agreement.

"Are you okay?" Michael asks, opening up my door.

"I'm fine," I sigh. "What are you doing in here?"

"I thought I heard voices. I just wanted to make sure you're okay."

"I was talking to Maggie."

"Do you think she can hear you?" he asks. "I swore Annabelle could. I always wished I had talked to her more during Jan's pregnancy...but I...it wasn't the best of situations."

"Maggie always moves and reacts. I like talking to her," I respond cautiously. When he talks about Annabelle and his life from the past it touches me deeply. I can feel his hurt and regret.

This is new. In North Carolina, Michael wouldn't even begin to talk about his past. Until that horrible night, I didn't even realize Annabelle was his daughter. I watch as he turns around. The pale light shining through the hallway bounces off of him, displaying his scars. *To me he is beautiful.* I sigh. I should let him go, and yet somehow, I can't stop my big mouth from opening. "It's four in the morning. How are you even operating? You just admitted earlier tonight you had been up all night and then today too."

"I'll rest tomorrow when Devil watches over you and Maggie. I don't want to risk sleeping and not hearing you call if you need me."

"Michael that's crazy. Go use the spare room and sleep. I'm fine. I'll scream loudly if I need you."

"Stop worrying about me, Beauty. I told you I'm fine."

"I thought I asked you to stop calling me that," I mutter.

"Sorry," he mumbles. "I'll just be outside," he says, going to the door again and I feel like an ass. I don't know why, but I think I hurt his feelings. Before I can second guess myself, I reach over and turn on the bedside lamp.

"I can't sleep," I confess, sitting up in bed, pulling the sheet up to my chest. "Today was surreal. I think maybe I'm a magnet for trouble, Michael." He stops and turns back to me. With the light on, I can see him clearer. His hair is long and unkempt, as always— but sexy, like a lover's hair that you've roamed your hands in over and over while he.... *Okay.* Best not to go there. I haven't had a problem with my hormones the last two months, I thought that part of pregnancy had worn off, especially since I'm as big as the side of a house. Apparently it only takes being within two feet of Michael. He doesn't help matters, wearing those jeans that hug him just right, a well-worn black t-shirt that clings to his muscles...*God.*

"You do seem to get into trouble from time to time," he almost laughs, walking towards me slowly and sitting down on the edge of the bed.

"Thank you for putting that nicely," I grumble and I watch as his lips slide into an unconscious smile.

"You need to rest, for Maggie's sake as well as your own," he says uncomfortably, as if he doesn't know how to talk to me one on one. I hate that we have this awkwardness between us now. I don't want it—I just have no idea what to do about it.

"The house is too quiet. I'm used to Clive's snoring," I say, just to have something to say. In response Michael grunts.

"I don't want to hear that shit."

"What?" I ask and I'm probably completely clueless because I have no idea what he's talking about.

"I don't like the idea of you living with someone else, Hayden. I sure as fuck don't want to hear about it."

"We didn't...but...Good Lord! You're insane. I didn't live with Clive, not like *that*."

"He cooked dinner for you, he lived in the same house as you —*alone*, for over a month," Michael replies.

"You are a moron. We're friends. He was hired to watch over me and I never would have met him if you hadn't forgotten to take your meds that night in the loft," I huff in return. Just when I was starting to soften to the big jerk, he has to remind me he's an idiot. Michael lets out a growl that would likely wake up my neighbors. I'll probably get complaints from the housing association.

"I'm not arguing with you at five in the morning, Hayden," he barks, getting up.

"It's four in the morning and if you'd stop being an idiot, we wouldn't," I respond in my own barking voice—which is nowhere as good as Michael's, but that's beside the point.

Michael rubs the bridge of his nose, holding his head down. "Why do women have to be so damn complicated?"

"It's one of life's mysteries. Just like me wondering why men have to be so pig-headed and stupid...Ow!" I end my mini tirade on a cry of pain.

"Are you okay, sweetheart? What's wrong?" Michael asks, his

anger immediately gone as he turns to me at the head of the bed and kneels down so he can see my face.

I sit completely still for a minute. I won't lie, that was an intense pain. It was in my back and it only lasted a couple of seconds, but it felt like someone was stabbing a hot knife into me. It was so bad that it took my breath away. I wait and nothing else happens.

"I think I'm okay. My back has been bothering me for a few days. Maybe I moved too fast or something," I tell him, trying to brush off his concerns and my own.

"I was worried you were going into labor, or something," he sighs, still looking concerned.

I rub my hand over my stomach and do my best to laugh it off. "Nope doodlebug isn't quite ready yet," I smile. Maggie picks that moment to push against my stomach around my belly button. "Whoa," I laugh as even the sheet moves.

"What is it?" Michael asks and without thought, I lower the sheet and grab his hand bringing it to my stomach where you can feel Maggie move the most. Maggie can feel the added weight of his hand because she kicks out harder. I laugh and look up at Michael's face. His eyes are warm with emotion and his face is etched in surprise. "She's strong," he said his voice thick and grainy.

"She is," I agree. I know I'm insane. I do. I should be panicking. Yet, right now in my bedroom with Michael beside me, Maggie moving under our combined touch I feel happy again. The kind of happy I haven't felt since that day on the lake with Michael. Michael. It's always...*Michael.* I let my thumb brush against the deep indented scar on his hand and in that moment I accept the inevitable. *I will always love Michael Jameson.*

## ❧ 12 ❧

## MICHAEL

"There's been no fucking word on Blade at all?" I growl into the phone. I'm getting frustrated. The bastard couldn't have just totally disappeared, but with all the club's resources and my own combined—there has still not been a sign of him. It's driving me crazy.

"None, amigo," Skull replies. "How are things going there?"

"They're...going," I sigh, rubbing the back of my neck in agitation.

"Your mujer, she is close, si? She will deliver soon," he adds and I heave out a breath that seems to drag from somewhere deep inside of me. *My woman.* A joke. I've been living with Hayden for two weeks. I thought I could handle it, I thought we would go back to the easy rapport we had before. It's not working out that way. In fact, we seem to spend most of our time being awkward with each other. The only part we manage to connect about is Maggie. She takes pleasure in letting me experience things with her and God, I do too. It's the first time I can remember that I haven't resented the fact there was a baby or child coming into the world that Annabelle couldn't stay in.

"According to her last doctor visit, she still has almost a month to go," I tell him. "I'd like Blade to be found before then. I need to make sure Hayden and Maggie are safe," I tell him. My plan was to make sure Blade was taken care of and then leave. The more time I stay with Hayden, the more that plan fades and a new one begins to form. One where I get to keep both her and Maggie in my life. Can I manage to control the anger inside of me to do that? *I have no fucking idea.*

"I'll keep Torch sending out feelers, hermano. Keep your head up and your eyes open."

"Will do. Later, man," I answer and I disconnect the call feeling strange. My relationship with Skull has been strained, to put it nicely. Most of it's on me, I freely admit it. There's so much water under the bridge, so many things that have happened, I know it will never go back to the way it was. I don't even mind it, which, I guess, makes me an even bigger bastard.

"Did you get a hold of him?" Hayden asks, coming back from the restroom. I look up to see her slide into the chair. We didn't attempt a booth because Maggie is definitely making her presence known these days. Hayden's stomach is stretched tight. It's no wonder her back is causing her problems. I don't see how she maneuvers things as gracefully as she does.

"Yeah. Still no word," I tell her with a sigh.

"I told you. Blade has put me out of his head. You guys are all being over protective for nothing. Maggie and I never meant anything to him. This is just crazy."

"Blade is unhinged. You can't figure out crazy and you sure can't trust it, Hayden."

"Whatever. I'm just saying this is pointless. You need to get on with your life. You don't need to try and keep some promise to keep me and Maggie safe. We're not your responsibility," she responds.

This argument isn't anything I haven't heard over and over for the last couple of weeks. It is however, one I'm getting tired of hearing. Since making myself known to Hayden, I have had one thought and it's a thought that keeps repeating, especially recently.

Can I somehow manage to control my anger enough so I can keep Hayden and Maggie? Is that possible? I feel calmer when I'm around them. I feel more like the person I used to be. Could I keep them? Hayden has a lot of her own anger directed towards me because of that night. I can't blame her. I'm actually surprised she's let me back in as much as she has. It's all a fucked-up mess in my head. I shouldn't even be contemplating any of this—not when I can't be sure I can keep control of my rage and not lash out like I did before. Still, I have hope. I can't stop the hope. These last two weeks...have been...*good*.

"What if I wanted you to be?" I ask her, before I can stop myself.

"To be what?" she asks, confused.

"To be my responsibility. What if I wanted you and Maggie back in my life?"

"I'd say you forgot your medication again and we both know how that goes," she answers, her face going white. "Waitress! Can we have our bill please?" she adds, which pisses me off, because we've barely set down and have only had our drinks.

"What are you doing? We're not ready to go. I'm hungry."

"Fine. Then you can stay and I'll grab a taxi."

"The hell you will, besides I doubt Nowhere, Wyoming has taxis. I sure haven't seen them. Quit trying to piss me off and figure out what you want for breakfast."

"I—"

"Don't bother denying it. We both know you're trying to make me angry, just so I'll be an asshole and you'll have more reason to keep that wall up between us."

"I don't think I need any more reasons than I already have," she huffs, her voice pouting.

"That's good, because I plan on tearing that fucking wall down brick by brick," I warn her.

"I don't know why," she sighs. "You should ask yourself one thing, Michael."

"What's that?"

"Why are you so anxious to tear down my walls and get my...get me..."

"Get you back in my bed?" I finish for her, watching her closely. Disappointment comes over her face and I have a feeling I answered something wrong—that I made some type of misstep. *Why does dealing with women always feel like I'm trying to navigate through a minefield?*

"Why do you want me there, when you had me there once and weren't satisfied until you pushed me out of it?" she asks, her voice quiet and sad.

I have no idea how to answer her. I'm a fucking mess. If she knew how much, maybe she would understand.

*Maybe I need to start letting her see just how fucked up I am. Will that make her push me away harder? Or would she be the one person to understand how broken I feel inside? Would she care? Would she stay? Can I do this?*

I've got too many questions about Hayden, and not one fucking answer. Worse...I don't know how to get the answers...at least not easily.

*Fuck.*

## ❦ 13 ❧

## HAYDEN

"**I**f we're going to learn to get along, Hayden. I think we need to put the past behind us," Michael says. I look across the table at him and sigh.

"Why can't you go back to grunting and not speaking? Remember that man? Be him again," I order, turning my attention back to the menu in my hand. I need to be smart here. Michael doesn't realize how much I want what we had back. I want it more every day I'm with him. The problem is, I don't think I could survive him leaving again. I need to keep myself together here because Maggie is depending on me.

Michael leans back against the green vinyl booth seat. We got a table that has a booth seat on one side and then regular chairs for me, because there's no way I can fit in the booth seat. Michael is so big and broad, I'm not sure how he does. Somehow he does, though he still looks almost freakishly big sitting there, giving me this solemn look. I know I've disappointed him, and I don't want that to bother me, but for some reason it does.

"See anything you like, Beauty?" he asks and I really need him to stop calling me that. I can't handle him being nice to me and using that name. I have to remain strong. I can't let him back in and survive. I. Just. *Can't*.

"Please stop calling me that, Michael," I sigh. "And I think I'll have the bacon omelet."

"No Bananas and peanut butter?"

"I doubt you can get that here, but no. That craving stopped a month ago. I don't really have cravings now. I just feel fat and tired all the time. The doctor readjusted my delivery date the last time I was there. I wanted to kill him. I waddle when I walk and I can't see my ankles, but I'm told they're swollen too," I rattle off. I'm nervous. Each minute that I'm in Michael's presence, I feel a little more of my willpower slip away.

"You're not fat. You—"

"Michael—" I start to warn him, and he holds his hand up to stop me from talking.

"How about we make a deal?" he says and he looks so sensible, so relaxed. I have warning bells going off in my head right now.

"What kind of deal?" I ask cautiously.

"I get to tell you one thing I think is important, and you have to listen without stopping me, without judging what I tell you. You have to take it on faith that what I'm telling you is the complete truth—because it is," he starts and I immediately shake my head no.

"How is that a deal?"

"You didn't let me finish, Beauty. In return, I promise to give you one thing that you ask for. Anything you want it doesn't matter, even if it is to buy you a hundred peanut butter and banana sandwiches," he shrugs.

"And you promise not to renege? You tell me one thing you think is important and in return I take it on faith and try to believe you and you have to do whatever I tell you to do?"

"Within reason. I'm not leaving you alone and unprotected, but yes anything else. And vice-versa."

"I like this idea," I tell him, thinking I could definitely use it to my advantage. He has to be getting something out of it, however.

There's a look in his eyes that makes me think I have to be very cautious. "Wait. What do you mean vice versa?"

"If you tell me something, then I get one favor from you," he says, and I want to laugh. This sounds easy, because I know beyond a shadow of a doubt that I don't want to tell Michael anything. I'm much safer not talking with him at all. "Oh, and I should say that if you want to ask me something, or I want to ask you something, the same rules apply." Okay that little add-on makes me very nervous.

"Ask?" I squeak out, and a nervous jerk moves through my fingers. Why this should terrify me, I'm not exactly sure, but it does.

"Exactly. If we ask one another questions, we have to answer honestly, but the reward will be the same."

"How often do we have to play this game?" I ask.

The waitress comes over and takes our order as I think over the conversation. I feel like I'm bargaining with the devil and I should stop. I have a feeling the devil always wins. Once the waitress leaves, Michael's eyes bore into me. *Am I imagining how intense he seems right now?*

"There's no limit."

"Oh no. No way in hell. There has to be a limit," I argue, immediately seeing scenarios where he is constantly asking me questions I don't want to answer and hounding me with them.

"Okay fine then. What do you suggest?"

"Once a day," I say emphatically.

"That seems awful safe of you. Come on Hayden, aren't there things you want to know about me, that I've never told you? Things you've wondered, but never asked?" he teases—and it tempts me. I have to remain steadfast here. *I have to.*

"Once a day, no more than twice," I respond, taking the bait. *Crap!*

Michael smiles, a big smile, one that reaches his eyes. He knows he's won. I've played into his hands. I don't know exactly how, but I have a sinking suspicion I will soon.

## ※ 14 ※

# BEAST

"**D**amn it!" I hear Hayden exclaim through the door. I instantly move to open it.

"You okay?" I ask, peering into the dark room. She's sitting up in bed, reaching behind her to touch her lower back.

"It's really getting creepy the way you're listening for sounds in my bedroom every night Michael," she sighs out. "My back is just cramping again."

"Pregnant women shouldn't mention cramping, because that sounds like contractions. Maybe we should take you to the doctor."

"It's not that. My back just hurts. I injured it once and it's always given me trouble."

"How did you injure it?"

"Dancing on tables at wild parties," she says, looking up at me with an '*I dare-you*' look.

"Funny, Hayden," I mumble, shaking my head. This woman never cuts me a bit of slack. "Here, let me see if I can help." I walk around the bed and sit down on the side opposite of where she's laying. Her eyes go wide, as the bed dips with my weight. She tenses and and grips the sheet as if her life depended on holding it.

"What are you doing?" she squeaks when I all but pick her up and position her horizontally on the bed.

"Stretch out on your side if you can, honey," I instruct, more than expecting her to argue. It surprises me when she doesn't. She does it without protest. A small whimper escapes when I touch her lower back. I'm no professional, but it doesn't take one to feel the knots in her muscles. "You need to relax more," I chastise, letting my hands slide under her t-shirt to begin kneading my fingers against her back. She seems to tense up even more at my touch. I do my best to ignore that and continue the massage. Eventually she stops holding her body so stiff and straight and relax into me. "Better?" I ask, enjoying the freedom to touch her. I've missed her, more than I've allowed myself to admit.

"You have magic fingers," she almost moans out. My fucking dick hardens and there's not a damn thing I can do about it. I wish I was wearing my sweats, because suddenly these jeans are damn painful.

"Glad you think so," I tell her with a laugh, wishing my fingers were elsewhere...*wishing they were inside of her.*

"I...uh...I didn't mean it like that," she mumbles.

"Trust me, I know," I answer, and damn if that doesn't almost make me sound like a child pouting. Still, she's been keeping me at arm's-length for so long, it's driving me crazy.

"I can't believe you're still awake. You're a freak of nature. You're going to pass out someday when everything catches up to you. Human beings cannot go without rest, Michael. It's just not natural."

"I'm not resting until—"

"Yeah, yeah. I've heard the song and dance. It's crazy. You're just in the next room."

"The next room can be too far away, if I need to be by your side quickly," I murmur, concentrating on the feel of her skin and how fucking good it feels to move my fingers over it.

"Clive stayed there just fine and nothing happened. What did Victor do to him anyways?"

"He had another job he needed him to work on," I tell her. Leaving out the fact that the job was in Germany—*and that it still wasn't far enough away from her*.

"And I can't rest without being able to see for myself if you're okay. When I have to crash, we have Devil—annoying as he is."

"He's something alright. He's got both D.D. and Jenn wrapped around his finger. God, that feels good. Thank you, Michael."

"My pleasure," I nearly groan. Thank God her back is turned to me, because I have to reach down and adjust my dick before my jeans cut the fucker in half. I need to steer this conversation—and my thoughts away from sex. *Quickly.* "Don't you have anything you want to ask me, Hayden? Anything at all?" I ask her. When I thought of this little game at the restaurant that day I thought it would be simple. I should have known that nothing is ever simple where Hayden Graham is involved. She didn't take the bait over lunch. She hasn't taken the bait in over two days. The damn woman is stubborn as hell. More so than I ever gave her credit for.

"All kinds of things," she shrugs, slyly looking over her shoulder at me. Her gray eyes are almost twinkling and this is as close to a smile as I've seen from her since that day at the diner. She's playing games with me now. She's taken this game as a challenge. She doesn't realize that two people can play that game.

"Then ask away, *Beauty*," I tell her, putting an emphasis on the name I've given her.

"Will you stop calling me that?" she growls, her voice taking on this grouchy quality that makes her sound like a mama bear protecting her cubs.

"Is that the fee you want for answering one of my questions?"

"You're unbelievable," she says shaking her head. "I'm going to take a shower and ignore you."

"If that's what you want to do, Beauty," I tell her flopping over on the bed, grinning when I hear her growl under her breath. I put my hands behind my head and try to think of some imaginary number. If I use the name Beauty often enough, she's going to take the bait. I just need to be patient.

"Okay fine," she huffs, and I jerk my eyes to her face. *Or not.* The thrill of victory runs through me. She gave in much easier than I thought she would.

"Fine?" I ask, wanting it spelled out.

"I'll play your stupid game. Do your worst, but when you're done you can't call me Beauty again," she all but demands. She's standing across from me now, at the foot of the bed where I'm lying. She's got both her hands crossed at her chest and those gray eyes of hers are glowing with anger. Her hair is down and ruffled from tossing and turning without sleep. Her soft pajama shirt is tight around her stomach and her breasts are even larger now than they were in North Carolina. She's never looked better. She calls to everything inside of me.

There's so many things I want to say to her, but even if she's giving in right now, I know she's not really ready to hear everything I want to tell her. I decide then, I have to go the easy route. Hopefully it will get her to where she feels comfortable doing this more often.

"Fine. You want me to stop calling you Beauty?"

"More than you could ever imagine," she says passionately, which if I'm honest annoys the fuck out of me.

I fight down that emotion though. I turn my body to face her, then reach behind me and grab some of her pillows. I grab two of the four pillows within easy reach and stuff them under my head for support. I lay there looking up at the most complicated, beautiful woman I've ever met. She's so different from anyone I've encountered. She has her own scars, her own demons and yet she's risen above them and came out of it all stronger. She's stronger now than she had been in North Carolina. Every day I'm with her I see new signs of that strength. "Got it. I'll stop calling you Beauty," I tell her, vowing somehow I will find a way to do it.

"What question do I have to answer," she sighs, looking like I'm about to kick her damn dog or something.

"None. I just want to tell you why I started calling you Beauty."

"I don't really—"

"Remember the rules, Hayden."

"Fine. Get it over with," she says and she doesn't realize how hard this is going to be for me. My palms are actually fucking sweating. My heart rate has kicked up in speed, but I stick to my guns. I want Hayden back. When Hayden is in my life, life is bearable. I can breathe without feeling like I'm drowning. I want to hold on to that. I need to. I'm desperate to. I just need to let Hayden in a little more and somehow suffocate this rage inside of me—at least enough so that it doesn't hurt her again.

"After Annabelle died, my world went black, Hayden."

"Michael..."

"And I don't mean that figuratively. It literally went black. You've seen the scars on my face, the ones my hair and beard don't conceal. I had to wear bandages, a fucking lot of them. The pain was so intense, that I was sedated and when the pain wasn't the reason...they would sedate me, because the grief and the anger would pour out of me in waves of rage that couldn't be controlled. So much of that time is a painful, dull haze." I've been looking at her, while I talk, but as the memories come back to me, my head goes down. I let myself think back and get lost in them. "Slowly I began to heal, but everything changed. My brothers would come in the room and they'd do their damnedest to act normal...but I saw. There was pity in their eyes. The conversations were stilted, where they never were before. I couldn't talk much, not then. It hurt too fucking much. The worst was when Briar and his old-lady would come in. They cared about me, I knew it, but here they were with their daughter, when I just lost mine. They would walk in, so deeply in love it clung to their skin, like a smell, a stink that slid inside of me and nearly destroyed me. They had everything. They were happy. They had love, they had their children... and I just lost my entire world. *My Annabelle was gone.* I hated them. I hated their daughter. Here was this innocent child, who was happy and loved by everyone—*completely innocent*...and I hated her. I hated her because she could breathe and laugh and grow. She could do all of those things and my daughter couldn't. Does that make me a monster, Hayden?" I ask, looking up at her, finally. "I hated an innocent child. It didn't even stop there. Months and months later, I would see a child and the hurt and anger would claw inside of me —like a living thing. It got worse when Skull's wife came back. It had been years, so you think I would have changed—*I hadn't*. I kept it hidden, but the rage and pain were still all there. Hell, I couldn't even stand to look at their daughter. I hated her, because her very existence was the reason my daughter died," I confess.

Hayden sits down on the bed and reaches out her hand so that it lays over mine. One by one her fingers slide into mine, and her thumb brushes against the largest scar there. Familiar. Calming. One of the biggest things I missed when she left was this... her hand in mine. My chest is tight from the memories, but I grasp her hand tightly—needing it like a lifeline.

"Give it to me, Michael," she whispers, confusing me. My eyes seek hers out, those gray depths are shining with unshed tears and staring straight at me. "Give it to me, all of it and then it's gone. Finish the story and we can start putting it behind you," she whispers, and a few of the tears overflow and fall from her eyes. My heart stalls. It's all there. The memories of what her and I shared. *She has them.* She's held onto them. She just gave me the very words I gave her all those months ago. *She remembers.* That gives me the courage to keep going.

"Once, at the club. We were fixing some concrete pads for a celebration the club was having. Skull came in with Gabby... It had been a bad day, Hayden. I try not to show it, but there are times, especially earlier on, when the muscles in my legs and arms are weak. Moments when the tightness of the skin...and the nerve endings close to the damaged muscles ache. I can't handle being around people when I'm like that. I don't know how else to explain it. I had worked all day and then went to a physical therapy appointment for issues I was having. I hated therapy. The therapists tried, but the more they touched me...the more work they made me do, the more I had to endure...I don't know how to explain it, other than it felt like every nerve ending in my body was being tortured. I wanted to scream, I wanted to lash out...I wanted to hurt someone...*So I did.*"

"What did you do? Finish it."

"I just got back to the club, and had crashed in the main room with a beer. Gabby came running in. She saw my burns and the scars, because I had taken my shirt off. The air conditioner was broken...."

"Finish it, Michael."

"Gabby got scared when she saw me. She started crying and it was just...*too much*. It became the edge of the cliff and I jumped without looking back. I screamed at Skull and Beth to leave. I screamed while staring at Gabby. I knew I was terrifying her, I knew I was making her cry, I knew it all and somewhere down deep...*I enjoyed it*," I confess, waiting for her to pull away and leave. To condemn me for being a monster. She doesn't. Instead, her hand tightens on mine. I stare down at it, watching as her thumb continuously brushes back and forth along a scar that once seemed so ugly, but now, with her touch feels...normal...fuck...it even feels good. *Calming.* "From that moment on, I embraced the blackness inside of me, Hayden. I let it swallow me fucking whole. I didn't care. I became a monster.

"Michael, honey—"

"There would be times I wanted to try and be like I used to be —move back into my old life. I mean all around me my club, my brothers were doing it. All around me they were laughing, having babies, living their lives, and they were happy. I wanted to be like that."

"But it wasn't possible," she whispers. I'm busy staring at our joined hands. I can't pull my eyes from them. If I do, I might stop, and I need to make her understand—if nothing else. I don't know if I'll get another chance, and I need her to understand...

"I tried, but something always happened. A memory of my daughter, doing the same things their kids would do. Watching as they kissed their wives, just something small like that. It would bring back the reality that I lived in."

"Because your family was gone," she injects quietly and she's mostly right, but it goes deeper than that, so I give her that too.

"My family was gone, but why would a woman want to be around a monster, Hayden? Why would a woman invite an animal, who was riddled in scars, who had a soul as black as midnight, and was slowly dying from the inside out...What woman would want a man like that to touch her?" Her hand constricts so forcefully on mine, it might hamper blood flow, but I like it. It feels solid. It feels reassuring. "There was a girl. I mentioned her before. She had this huge crush on me for as long as I could remember. She was sweet, innocent and all the things I had never had in my life. I never let myself act on it. There was Jan, and she might have been a cold hearted bitch, but I needed to put Annabelle first, but still I knew this girl cared and...*I liked it.* I had been making progress, trying to come out of my head in small moments and interact with my brothers. There was a family picnic. All the brothers and their families were there and I was really trying. I was. It was all fake, but I was surviving being around everyone. That was an improvement...and then I heard her and the other girls talking—about me. She didn't say anything I didn't already know. Still..."

"You told me," Hayden murmurs. "She was a—"

"A cow and other colorful things. I remember, Beauty," I smile, bringing my free hand over our joined ones and just holding it there. Letting the feelings inside of me settle. "She wasn't wrong though. I was repulsive."

"You were—*are* not. Michael, you can't let close-minded—"

"I was," I interrupt her. "I absolutely was, inside where they couldn't see. I was repulsive. One of my brother's was celebrating the birthday of his son, and Skull was too...and through the whole party I was trying to act normal—*be normal*. It was all fake. I wanted to scream at them and demand to know why their sons got to live and my daughter couldn't? I wanted to know what made them so special that they got to have time with their families, they got everything that had been taken from me. You see, Beauty? I wasn't normal. I was never going to be normal. Lucy was right that day. I'm repulsive."

## ❧ 15 ❧

## HAYDEN

I can't catch my breath. My heart is hurting so deeply for Michael. There's so much to process and I'm trying to do it in short bursts, but he keeps giving me more and with each new detail, I'm robbed of air. This isn't something I can digest and ignore. This will take days to truly understand and I want to understand. I need to know the hell that Michael has been locked inside. I need to, because as much as I try to run...I want Michael for keeps. I want him to stay and as stupid as it sounds, someday I hope he will come to care about me. I have so many questions. What did he mean when he said Jan was a bitch? What happened with Lucy? Was he able to talk to Skull and Beth? Did he tell Briar how stupid and thoughtless it was for him to bring children in to see him? Did that entire club have no idea of the pain and misery Michael was living with? Did they not get that they were adding to it? I bite my lip and try to keep concentrating on nothing but Michael. This is important. In this story there is something I really need to know.

"Do you still...do you still resent..." *Crap.* I'm messing it up. I don't know how to ask what I want to know, because I'm scared of the answer.

"Do I resent Maggie?" he asks, showing me he understands. I hold my head down in shame. I hate that I asked him that, but at the same time I need to know.

"Yes," I breathe the word quietly, so quiet you can barely hear it.

"I can't lie, Beauty. I did. Then, slowly, Maggie became something else. She became hope." I look up at him then, waiting for him to explain. *Needing him to.*

"Hope?"

"Before I met you, I told you the world had changed for me. I was being swallowed by the blackness inside of me. Somehow you, even against my will, managed to get under my skin. You taught me how to breathe, how to take in clean air. Holding you in my arms, hearing your laugh, sliding inside your body, I didn't feel the black as much anymore. I felt hope. I saw...*beauty.* You gave that back to me, Hayden. That's why I call you Beauty, because you gave it to me again. When I didn't think I would ever see or feel it again, you gave me beauty."

He's said so much for me to take in. Michael's words slide inside of me in a way I know I'll never be able to let it go. If I was smart I would run away right now, push Michael away anyway I can. He's injured deeply inside and the damage is so intense, I'm not sure it can ever be repaired. I know more than anyone that life doesn't give you happy endings. Everything inside of me is screaming for me to run. Instead I pick up one of the extra pillows, pull it into my lap, and reluctantly take my hand away from his.

"Hayden?" he asks, and I can hear the concern and anxiousness in his voice. I keep my head down and close my eyes for a minute. I just need to give myself time to pull my reactions in. "Hayden?" he prompts again.

I let out a large breath. My mind is a mess. My emotions are a *bigger* mess. My mind keeps repeating over and over, *"Pull away, pull away."* My heart is demanding something else entirely. I slide off the bed, clutching the pillow as if it was a lifeline. Finally, I bring my head up to look at him and before I can stop them, words come out. Words that probably should never be spoken. Words that might prove my downfall.

"You can keep calling me Beauty," I tell him, completely giving in against my better judgment. I watch as shock streaks across his face as clear as day. He expected me to run. *I* expected me to run. Slowly I watch as one by one the shadows of the memories he had been discussing begin to fade. It's like watching the sunset. *Beautiful, poignant and breathtaking.*

"So I don't have to pay a fee this time?" he asks, and his eyes are sparkling. He looks younger like this. He's attractive—even fascinating. *Terrifying. He's terrifying.*

I toss the pillow at him and sigh, "You can sleep on the floor tonight. That will be your fee."

"The floor?"

"You said you can't rest in another room. So, sleep on the floor," I mutter, blushing and trying to avoid his eyes.

"There's a bed here."

"*My bed.*"

"It's a big bed, Hayden."

"It's not *that* big, Michael," I tell him shaking my head.

He growls in complaint, but before he can try to talk me out of it. I escape to the bathroom and close the door on him. I lean against it hoping I didn't just make a huge mistake...*and being terrified that I did.*

## ❧ 16 ❧

## BEAST

"What is that?" Hayden demands when she comes out of the shower. This probably won't go easy, but nothing ventured, nothing gained at this point.

"Pillows," I tell her trying to act like I have no idea why she's upset. I put my hands behind my head and wait. I'm also trying to act like my dick isn't pushing against the fabric of the gym pants I changed into. Lying here in Hayden's bed, her sheets heavy with the aroma of vanilla and sugar—*smelling like her*—has my balls so tight I could come at the slightest touch.

"I know they're pillows, Michael. What I don't understand is why you have so many of them on my bed."

"There's not a lot of them. I was only able to find nine."

"Nine is a lot of pillows, Michael. Wait...where are my pillowcases?"

Hayden is towel drying her hair, running the towel through her darkened tresses, in a way that makes me wish it was my fingers. She's wearing a long night shirt this time that comes way below the knee and is long-sleeved. It's a pale blue color with a giant bear in pajamas emblazoned on it, underneath it says, *"Dreamer."* It's adorably cute and a hundred percent Hayden. Jan would have never been caught dead in something like that. She had an entire closet full of expensive, lacy, shit and none of it was half as sexy as Hayden's nightshirt. Then again, it's all about the woman wearing it.

"You said Stroker slept in that spare room," I shrug, distracted because I'm wishing her shirt was shorter.

"So?" she asks, her brow furrowed in confusion.

"The fabric stunk of his cologne. He's not getting in this bed, Hayden—in any way. I put them in the washer."

"He's not...You put them in..." she shakes her head back and forth as if she can't believe it. Maybe I went overboard, but I don't give a fuck. I don't want that fucker here—not even his memory. "You know you're certifiably insane don't you?" she grumbles, and in answer I grunt. "Why are all the pillows on my bed?"

"Your floor is cold."

"What?"

"And hard."

"I don't think I'm following you."

"You want me to rest. I can't rest on the floor and you're right. I am tired. So, I came up with an alternate plan."

"An alternate plan?"

"I'll sleep here with you, on the bed, but I won't touch you. Instead we'll have a wall between us."

"A wall?" she asks and it might be wishful thinking, but I think I see a smile starting to form.

"Yeah."

"A wall of...*pillows*."

"That's the idea."

"If I wasn't so tired, I'd argue with you, but we have maybe an hour until daylight and I'm exhausted," she says and the ghost of a smile is gone. Now, I see nothing weariness.

"Come sleep, Beauty. I'll make sure you're safe."

"Michael...I'm not sure this is a good idea..."

"I won't touch you. I promise all we'll do is sleep. You'll be safe on your side of the pillows," I assure her, carefully keeping on my side to disguise my rock-hard cock. If she saw that she really would be worried.

"I'm going to have to buy more pillows tomorrow," she mutters under her breath, but it makes me smile. Then, she slides into her side of the bed, reaches over and turns out the lamp. She turns over giving me her back. I thought this would make me feel better, but right now it's just a reminder of what I used to have and pushed away. I let her see a glimpse of me earlier. She's still here, and unless I'm deceiving myself, she's not as closed off. Maybe she can handle all the twisted mess inside of me. For the first time in months, I'm hopeful. I roll over so my back is to her too. Maybe if I don't see her, I might be able to resist touching her. *Maybe.*

"I don't think I like your game, Michael. You got your way all the way around. You were supposed to give me what I wanted and I think you got what you wanted. Seems you still owe me."

"I think that's where you got it wrong, Beauty."

"How's that? You're in my bed, and you're *still* calling me Beauty."

"Yeah, but if I had my way, there would be no fucking pillows right now, Hayden. There would be you in my arms and me between your legs, buried inside of you." I've probably said too much. I need to rein it in, but I figure I might as well be honest with her.

I hear her soft exhale of breath. I feel the bed move as she moves. Covers pull in her direction as she seems to burrow under them. I figure she's going to ignore what I said, and that's okay —*for now.*

"I'm pregnant Michael. Extremely pregnant. I don't think that's possible right now," she whispers.

"Trust me, Beauty. I'd find a way," I grin.

"Goodnight, Michael."

"Night, Hayden," I respond and when I close my eyes...*I'm still smiling.*

# HAYDEN

"I can't believe you haven't attacked that man yet. Girl are you crazy? How long have you been without the D?" D.D. asks. I swear my manager, and probably best friend in the world, has sex on the brain. Not that I don't since Michael has come back. We've been sleeping in the same bed now for a week. Seven *long* days. Seven long frustration filled days! He's been true to his word too. He hasn't touched me and I kind of hate him for it. If he had been the one to initiate it, I wouldn't feel guilty. I could claim I got swept up in the moment. Which is total bullshit, and just me being a big chicken, but it's true.

"I don't want to talk about it," I grumble.

"But look at him out there, Hayden! Women are eye-fucking him like crazy and yet he still sits and stares at the door waiting for you to come back through it."

I sigh as I glance at the small two-way glass window that allows us to look out, but prevents the customers from seeing in. She's right. Michael's intense stare is on the door, nowhere else. She's also right about that damn redhead in the store. She's pretending to look at cupcakes and instead she keeps looking at Michael. He either doesn't notice or is just ignoring her. Either way, he's not giving her the time of day.

I'm voting that he doesn't notice. He has some serious issues about his scars, which is crazy because he's beautiful! That's what most women notice. I will admit there have been a few that stare at his scars and curl their nose in distaste. My first instinct has always been to throat punch them, but I don't want to draw attention to it, in case it bothered Michael. It's unbelievable that I'm trying to protect his feelings when I should be pushing him out of my life. Instead, I'm enjoying him back in my life and if I was being brutally honest, I also love having him back in my bed—*even without the sex.* I do miss the sex, though—a lot—and if I don't quit dreaming about it, Michael's going to know exactly how much.

"Let it go, D.D. Don't you have more important things to worry about? Like the East Side Elementary cupcake order, for example?"

"Yes, boss," she answers, rolling her eyes. We're both smiling, and even when she's being annoying, I still love her. "Hey, Hayden?"

"Yeah?"

"Since you're not claiming that man out there it probably doesn't matter, but..."

"But?"

"I think the redhead finally has his attention," she answers.

I can't stop myself from jerking around to look. Sure enough, the redhead is standing by Michael's side. She's practically pushing her breasts into his face when he finally turns around to look at her. I growl because even though it's not what I had planned, I find myself walking into the other room. I could lie and say I don't have a reason, but I know I do. It's to make sure that fake-boobed ginger stays away from my man. I let out a pent-up breath at that thought, because I realize what I just did.

*My man. You're a stupid, stupid girl Hayden Graham.*

"You look so familiar! I've been staring at you, trying to place you, Finally, I thought, oh shoot! I'll just ask!" the overzealous red-head chirps out, and her voice is almost nasally and very annoying.

"I don't think so," Michael all but grunts, which makes me smile. I pretend to be busy collecting baking sheets and spare a glance over at him. He's looking at me, those dark eyes intense and heated enough that it causes goosebumps to rise on my flesh.

"But a man like you, so virile and...." She pauses. In my head, I have to ask if this chick is for real. *Virile?* "And big," she finishes and she gasps the next word out like she's actually holding his damn cock. I might take my anger out on my baking pans by tossing them on the counter. They land *loudly*. The sound of them clanging together echoes through the small storefront. The woman jumps at the noise. "Goodness!" she complains. I raise my head up to look at her and Michael—and sure enough her boobs are still in his face. She has her hand on her chest in mock surprise at the noise I made, but you would have to be stupid not to realize she was trying to draw his attention to her tits. *How does one survive with that much silicone injected into their body?*

"Sorry," I huff. "There seems to be a pesky bug in here. It annoyed me," I grumble, turning to go in the back again, I've had about all of this I can stand. I stop short though when I hear it. Michael's laughter and it's honestly the first time he's laughed this loudly, this fully since that day at the lake. I can hear...*joy* in it. *It's beautiful. It's amazing.*

"A bug? How disgusting! Maybe you and I should—Oh my God!" the red-head screeches. "What happened to your face?" she all but yells, and just like that Michael's laughter stops. It stops and his face closes up. Suddenly, I hate that redhead for entirely different reasons. I want to slap her. It's my first instinct. The only thing that stops me—and it barely does—is the fact that I'm heavily pregnant. Instead, I march over and push her away from Michael.

"Get out!" I growl and not quietly.

"What? Why?"

"This is my bakery and I don't want you here. So get out."

"What is your problem?"

"My problem is that you were acting like a tramp and flirting with my man and then—"

"Your man?" Michael and the redhead say this together. I feel heat swamp me, but I don't give into it.

"Don't worry, honey. I'm not after him. Not after I got a good look at him. But, if I wanted to, I could definitely take him from you. Here's some advice for you. If you want to keep a man, you should at least try and do something with your hair—even if you do look like an elephant right now."

"You bitch," I growl, and I want to go after her and deck her. Pregnant or not, I think with one good hit she'd go down. I sure as hell am willing to try. Michael stops me however. He grabs my hand and pulls me. I land awkwardly on his lap. His hand comes up under my hair and he holds my neck.

"Your man?" he growls again.

"Michael—" I start, and I'm beginning to fear my outburst because I can see the depth of the heat and emotion shining in his eyes. My brain is crying, *"Retreat!"*

"Your man," he growls. "You claimed me, Hayden," he says, his voice dark and stormy. The look of victory in his eyes is so intense, my heart begins slamming against my chest. He brings our heads slowly together, his forehead resting against mine. His hand tight on my neck in a possessive hold. I want to run away. I want to deny it. I want to hold him forever. I close my eyes and try to breathe through the panic.

"I claimed you," I whisper—more to myself than to him. My hands find his hair, which he's wearing down today, and I hold onto it even while moving to cradle the side of his face. I open my eyes slowly. "I love you, Michael," I whisper, giving him words he might not want to hear—but the words that I can't contain, especially when I see the emotions on his face. He groans and the vibration of it seems to quake through my body. Leaving me hungry, needy for him and...*wet*. His lips come down on mine—rough, not gentle. He takes my mouth, his tongue thrusting inside my mouth to plunder and wage war. A war he's already won. A war I'm happy to surrender to. I'm so lost in the kiss that I don't even hear the woman leave. I hear nothing, except the pounding of my own heart. I'm pretty sure I'm crying. I can feel the tears slide from my eyes. Yet, they're not tears of sadness. *Not this time.*

All I feel is happiness, because after months of being alone, I finally feel like I'm whole again.

## ❧ 18 ❧

## BEAST

"Damn Sunshine, I think you might get lucky tonight," Devil laughs, interrupting my kiss with Hayden. She immediately stiffens in my arms and tries to pull away. I don't let her at first, needing just one more hit from her lips, one more chance to taste her. I soften the kiss, giving it to her gentle and sweet, nipping at her lips and sucking them into my mouth, teasing her with my tongue. Eventually, we break apart. I kiss along the side of her face to find her ear.

"Tonight, you're mine," I half-warn, half-promise. She jerks in my arms.

"I'm pregnant. *Really* pregnant," she answers, and her voice almost squeaks. She's acting so shy; my cock is crying to be inside of her right now.

"And fucking beautiful," I tell her with a growl. I can't resist kissing the side of her neck, raking my teeth roughly against the skin and marking her—not much but enough. Her fingers bite into my back, before she slowly pulls away and stands. She stares at me for a minute and I wonder if she's going to say anything else. She wrings her hands nervously.

"You want some coffee?"

"I'm good," I tell her gruffly. Fuck. I'm better than good.

"Devil?" she asks, suddenly remembering there's more than just me and her in the room.

"I'm good, sugar," he says, and she nods, gives me one last look and then leaves the room. I watch her walk away. I couldn't pull my eyes away if I tried.

"You are one lucky motherfucker," Devil says and I grunt my reply. Not exactly arguing with him. Right now, I agree. It's a strange feeling.

"What are you doing here?"

"About that," he says and something in his voice alerts me, and I pull my eyes away from the now closed door to look at him.

"There's been a mess at the club, Sunshine. I hate to leave you alone, but it seems quiet here and I'm needed—"

"What happened?"

"Someone waylaid Diesel. He was coming back from Knoxville with his boy and he says a cop was stopping traffic, or he thought it was a cop. They knocked him out and took his son."

"Fuck. Is it the same people who tried that shit before?" I growl, because Diesel's had this problem before. His fucking ex, Vicky, is always trying to take their child back. Ryan was born hooked on drugs, thanks to his mom. Diesel kicked her to the curb when he found out, and he's fought like hell to keep custody of his boy. He's managed, but it's been a battle.

"We think so. Diesel remembers hearing Vicky's voice before he lost consciousness."

"He okay?"

"Someone fucked him up pretty good. Slammed him across the head with a steel pipe."

"Fuck."

"So as much as I love our time together, Sunshine, I need to be heading out. You going to be okay?"

"Yeah. I'm good. I need anything I know where you are."

"Or you could call Skull. They still care about you brother. Once family, always family," he says, reaching out his hand. I take it, even if part of me doesn't want to. He doesn't get it, maybe no one else will, but I've had too much taken from me. There's too much water under the bridge. My days as a Devil's Blaze patched member are over. Even if I could get past the anger. There are too many memories back at the clubhouse. Too many memories are attached to that life. *And then there's Hayden.* She'd never want to live as an old lady. She wouldn't want to go back to that world, even if this club was different from the one that haunts her memories. What's more is, I wouldn't want to subject her to it.

"Keep in touch, brother," I tell him, because I do like him and maybe it's because he's not attached to my past. Whatever it is, he does feel like a brother.

"Will do." He says as we grab hands and thump backs. He turns to leave, before he goes out the door he turns to look at me. "Keep your ass dry and your dick wet, Sunshine."

Christ. I really don't understand why I like him.

But I do.

## ❧ 19 ❧

## HAYDEN

"Michael..."

"Hayden, don't," Michael responds and I exhale a breath and try to still my hands—which are currently clasping each other tightly and resting on my really *large* stomach. What was I thinking? I can't have sex. I can't do this.

"Michael, I...that is, we can't...*Crap!* I just don't think this is a good idea."

"It's going to happen, Beauty. If not tonight then tomorrow, or the next one, or a week from now. Either way it's going to happen. Does it really matter when?"

My brow furrows at his words. "Are you basically saying, we might as well get it over with?"

"Quit trying to pick a fight, Hayden. I get you're nervous about this, but—"

"With good reason!" I grumble back at him. In response, he gru-wls, which is what I've decided to call it when he grunts and growls at the same time. He moves his hand over his beard, like I've seen him do a million times. His eyes look up to the ceiling like he's praying for patience and then he looks back at me.

"Take off your dress."

"You can't be upset—wait—*What?*"

"Take off your dress, Hayden," he orders and it's definitely an order, there's no way you could mistake it for a request. He's also pulling his t-shirt over his head at the same time. I haven't seen him without a shirt in months. He's always kept one on, even when sleeping behind his pillow wall.

"Stop that! You can't get undressed!" I stumble through the words, almost to the point of stuttering. If he strips, I know my feeble defenses will be dust.

"I'm not fucking you with clothes on, Hayden. Now get out of that dress."

"I'm not taking my dress off. You can't...we can't do that. It's not possible," I respond, and I know I'm blushing. I can feel so much heat coming from my cheeks that it's a wonder I don't spontaneously combust.

"Fine," he answers with a shrug. I'm momentarily distracted because he's finished taking his shirt off and when he moves his shoulders, I can't help but watch how the rest of him moves. His skin glistens on the side closest to me. His pecs move slowly, almost like a gentle dance, and his six-pack of abs all follow the same subtle movement. His side with the scarring is starkly different, but to me, no less beautiful. The scars make this swirling, angry pattern on him, but it doesn't detract from his looks. In fact, knowing the story of how he got them, makes them almost tragically beautiful. I've never met a man in my life who would be willing to lay down his life for anyone. He must have loved his daughter so much. I wish I could have seen them together. My heart mourns his loss, but at the same time I know a profound sadness for the fact that Annabelle, with the beautiful blue eyes, will never get to experience the love of a father like that. The kind of love every child should have...*the kind I never got. The kind I pray Maggie gets to experience someday.*

"Fine?" I ask, trying to get out of the mini-trance that his body put me in. I'm letting my fingernails bite into the skin of my palm, in an effort to try and help—*it's not working*. Especially when my eyes drop down and his big hands are slowly unbuttoning his jeans. *Sweet Mercy...how can that simple thing be so hot and sexy?* It gets better though when he unzips his pants. That's it. He doesn't take them off but he unzips them. They slide low on his hips and he's not wearing anything underneath. They gape open in the front. I can see curls of dark hair, and a few inches of his hard shaft, with its ridges of veins pushing out against the darker skin. It's curved down, the remaining inches and head of his cock completely hidden by the dark denim of his jeans. My heart nearly stops and turns over in my chest, and I lick my lips, as I imagine pulling his dick out and running my tongue along it...I've never done that. Blade wasn't an oral type of person—at least with me. He got plenty of blow jobs from the club girls—*not that I knew that at the time.* With me it was strictly hard and fast sex for him. It was never really good to be honest. Being with Michael opened my eyes to *a lot.*

"I'll just rip the dress off of you," he grins, like that's the most normal thing in the world.

"What? Uh...No. I like this dress," I tell him, fear suddenly pulling me out of the stupor I was in.

"Hayden—"

"Michael, I'm not comfortable having sex...not with being so far along and things," I tell him with complete honesty.

He looks me over, and his forehead gets that little crinkle that it always gets when he's thinking about something. "Did the doctors tell you that you shouldn't have sex?" he asks, his voice going soft, as his hand comes up to curl around the side of my neck.

"What? No. I mean I didn't ask them because you weren't in the picture and it didn't seem necessary, but they said everything was fine and to resume normal activities during my checkup last week. I guess sex is normal..." I trail off when I watch the smile that moves over his face and nerves attack again. "But I mean I don't have long to go and...."

"Kiss me, Beauty," he interrupts, his voice dropping down low into my favorite timbre. My body takes that small step towards him, without me even realizing it. The minute I do his arms go around me. I feel them bite into the cheeks of my ass. My hands grasp his biceps and my fingers bite into the rock-hard, solid flesh. I use the hold to steady myself, while I try to pull myself from this magnetic hold he has on me.

"Michael. I'm not sure I forgive you, yet."

"But you want me," he counters—and *he's not wrong*.

"We have so much between us still, Michael," I try again.

"I know... clothes," he jokes. *He actually jokes.* His eyes sparkle with a mixture of heat and I think I see a trace of happiness. Have I seen that in him before? Maybe a quick flash, but this is different —this *feels* different.

"I'm huge..." I tell him, trying another tact as a Hail Mary because everything inside of me is urging me to take what he's offering. I miss sex...No. That's wrong. I miss, *Michael.*

"You're perfect," he corrects me and something about the way his fingers are moving along my neck with his thumb brushing against the side of my face, makes me believe him.

"You say that now but what happens if I go into labor in the middle of...*you know*..."

"You said the doctor said you aren't due for another month, now right? Plus, it's your first baby. First time mothers always deliver late."

"You have an answer for everything, don't you?"

"All but one thing," he agrees—smile still in place. His hands slide to my back and I can hear the sound of the zipper sliding down on my dress. He's unzipping it painfully slow and with each inch he reveals, the heat in his eyes intensifies. My heart is pounding in my chest and my mouth is dry. "I can't figure out why you're still dressed, Beauty."

"Don't hurt me, Michael," I plead, as he finishes, and my dress begins falling off my shoulders.

*I hope he understands I'm not talking physically...*

## ❦ 20 ❦

## BEAST

Before I met Hayden, I had forgotten what it felt like to take clean air into my lungs. After she left the darkness began slowly draining away all of the light she gave me. It was like taking away the sun. As I slowly back away from her and watch as her dress falls, revealing her body to me, I feel the light. *I feel the warmth*. Hayden is my sun...

Her dress falls revealing her body to me. Maybe some men wouldn't find her sexy, with her stomach tight, carrying a child. To me she is the most beautiful woman in the world. Everything Hayden does is done with her heart. I look at her face. She's blushing a bright pink and I see how nervous she is. She's practically broadcasting it. I need to take her mind away from the past, away from her being anything but the woman I want.

I drop to my knees in front of her.

"Michael, what are you..." she stops talking when I kiss her stomach. She bites into her lip as if to keep more words from coming out. I let my hands brush against the sides and kiss it again, right along the navel. My hands on her skin look wrong. Too dark to her light, too scarred for her milky white complexion.

"So beautiful, Hayden. You like this...you're performing a miracle. Giving life to a child, nurturing it with your body, and you're doing it with joy. You are a true beauty...I love everything about you," I whisper against her stomach. I move my hands down to her hips, hooking my fingers under the rim of her panties.

"Michael," she breathes softly, nerves still thickly laced in her voice.

I kiss down her stomach until I reach the blue silky material covering her from me. I place a kiss against the fabric, right at her center. I can't stop myself from inhaling and taking the scent of her excitement into my lungs.

"Are you wet for me, Beauty?" I ask her, already knowing she is. She whimpers without giving me an answer, but then none was needed. I can see evidence of it by the deeper hue on her panties. Unable to wait to see more, I grab the lacy strip of material that runs across her hips and rip it in half. One more tear and I'm able to pull them clean from her body, all with her standing still. I growl out, at what I reveal. It sounds like a bear when its mate is in view. The lips of Hayden's pussy are plump and shining with her sweet liquid. She's not just wet for me—she's drenched. "Perfect," I mumble, barely containing my hunger. My hands hold her hips, so large compared to her that they span her hip and thigh easily while my fingers dig roughly into the lush skin of her ass. I pull her body into me, using my tongue to slide against her lips and push inside of her.

"Michael..." she whispers. Her fingers wrap tightly in my hair, pulling my tongue deeper inside of her. I bring my hand down to open her further. I flatten my tongue out and leisurely slide it slowly across her pussy—beginning to end. I gather her juices as I go, not stopping until I reach her clit. She has haunted me these past months. I've lived and relived every single detail I've shared with her, but somehow her sweet, velvety taste is better than I remembered. I groan as I swallow it down and the flavor of her coats my mouth. "Michael it's been too long...I can't...I need to come, baby," she exhales the words out. They're quiet, but emotional. They float down to me. I doubt she has any idea the gift she's giving me. It's more than her body. It's the fact that it's me her body craves. Her quiet voice calling me baby, her hands in my hair, the reaction she had in the store to that woman...*All of it.* It's like food to a starving man. I once thought Hayden taught me to breathe again. Now, I know the truth. She's teaching me to live. Only, I don't want to do it without her. *I can't.* I won't try. Not again. I suck her clit into my mouth, using my tongue to dance across it, tease it, to fucking own it. Hayden leans heavily into me, her legs all but bending as she cries out. I want to see her, but there's no way I'm going to stop what I'm doing. I need her coming all over my face.

I take my hand that's still pulling one side of her juicy little cunt and move my fingers down in search of her entrance. I make sure they're slick with her come and I push two of them inside of her. I don't go far, just up to my knuckles. I've forgotten how fucking tight she is and the way she instantly clamps down to ride the hell out of my fingers. I need my cock in her. God I need her strangling my shaft as she comes.

I pull away, just for a second, long enough to look up at her face. Her head is thrown back, with her hair falling down in waves behind her like a waterfall. Her lips are parted and she's moaning my name over and over, so quietly I didn't realize it till just now. The sight causes that familiar pang to hit my chest. I didn't appreciate it before—I do now.

*I own Hayden's body. She's given it to me. She's mine.*

"Come for me, Beauty," I growl needing to give her more pleasure. Needing to remind her not to give up on me, the only way I can. I push my fingers in deeper, pulling them apart, readying her for our next round, because there's no way I'll be able to stop with just this. I need her too much. I suck her clit into my mouth, capturing it between my teeth, all while my fingers are fucking her relentlessly. She explodes the minute I put the slightest pressure on her clit, bathing me in her come.

I was right. She *is* teaching me to live. This is the first time I've felt my heart beat freely in months.

# 21

# HAYDEN

I feel like I'm floating. It takes me a minute to realize that I'm in Michael's arms and he's carrying me towards the bedroom. I should stop this. I won't survive if he lashes out at me again, but I don't want to stop it. The only two things I want in this world are Maggie and Michael. I shove the fear aside and curl into his arms, kissing his shoulder. I'm surprised when he brings his head down to kiss the top of my head. It makes me smile. I touch his soft beard, letting my fingertips disappear into the dark hair. I find the spot he always scratches and find the dark groove of the scar there. I let my fingers dance over the ridge carefully. I feel a tremor run through his body. For a moment, I'm worried that I've upset him, and I start to take my hand away.

"Sorry," I whisper.

"I like it," he grunts out and the deep sound of hunger in his voice, can't be denied, so I continue playing. When we get to the bed he lays me on it like I'm something extremely valuable and precious. It seems like irony that he lays beside our wall of pillows —one that obviously didn't work well. He throws them on the ground impatiently and then straightens to look down at me. "You're beautiful, Hayden," he says again and I grin, thinking he's starting to sound like a broken record. I realize he's doing it to make me believe it. I'm not sure that's ever going to be possible, but the thing is, when he says it...*I'm starting to believe he thinks it.*

"Is it alright to admit I'm nervous about this—despite what just happened?"

"Do you want me to stop?"

"No," I tell him, unable to articulate any further, because all the things I want to say are clogged inside of me. I can't say them to him because it might make me sound like a fool—or end in me begging him to love me.

"I'll be gentle, Beauty. We'll go as slow and as easy as you want. I just...need to be a part of you again," he confesses, his eyes never leaving my face. I might have been able to resist anything else. *Maybe.* But, the way he says that, unleashes something inside of me...something that has been holding me back from giving myself to Michael fully. What woman could remain strong, when the man she's in love with tells her he needs to be part of her. This is deeper than just sex.

"I want that too," I tell him, my voice heavy with emotion and the moment so important to me that I can feel tears forming. Being pregnant makes me cry at the drop of a hat, but this is more...this is *important.* My breath stalls as he pushes his pants from his hips. They were already hanging so low you could see a dark thatch of hair, but when they fall from him, they reveal just how amazing he is. Even scarred he still reminds me of a Greek god. All hard lines and perfectly defined areas that are this golden hue as if the sun has kissed every inch of him. His scars never bothered me, except that I know they were painful for him. How any woman could look upon them and not love them, especially since they are a symbol of the type of man he is, is beyond me. Right now I can't devote time to even thinking about them, because I'm suddenly remembering how huge Michael is and how being with him might be challenging right now.

"I'll be gentle," he confirms again, and I think that means my fear shows on my face. I try to swallow it down. I know Michael would never hurt me—not like that. He's always been gentle with me, even in the heat of sex.

"I know," I assure him, and I do. He gets on the bed, instantly positioning himself over me. Michael's the only man in the world that would make me feel small—especially right now.

I watch as he sits back on his knees, between my legs. He takes his shaft in his hand and I have to bite my lip to keep from moaning out at the erotic picture he makes. He strokes himself slowly, looking down at my body as if I'm a prize from a war he has waged. My body thrusts up toward his, almost against my will. I can't look away as I watch pre-cum gather on the massive head of his cock.

"Hungry, Beauty?" he half-laughs. He has no idea, not really. In answer I use my legs to pull myself down on the bed a little, pulling myself closer to him. I bend my knees, keeping my legs spread wide to allow him room. In response, a smile spreads on his face, causing that crinkle I adore around his eyes. "That's my girl," he murmurs, right before he moves the head of his cock against my pussy. I cry out. There's no way I could stop it when the head of his shaft slides against my clit. Back and forth, and then down to my entrance. He pushes just the head of his cock inside and somehow it only emphasizes how empty I am without him.

"Please, Michael," I beg. "Stop teasing me."

"Give me your hand," he orders, and his voice is so gruff, so full of hunger that it's just as erotic as what he's doing to my body. I look up and his face is intense. I reach out to him and his hand connects with mine. Our palms meet and his heat instantly invades my body. His fingers thread through mine and we join hands at the exact time he pushes in, joining our bodies.

"God yes. I've missed you, Michael."

"Don't let me go too far, Hayden," he says and it's then that I realize, he's inside of me, but not as deep as when we were first together. He's holding back to protect me—to protect Maggie. It can't be easy for him either. If anything was left of that feeble wall I tried to keep between us, this just destroyed it. I feel him moving in and out of me and I start to reassure him I'm fine, but then I see the moment he starts to go over the edge. He begins moving in me faster and faster. His other hand comes down to find my clit and I shatter. I feel him follow me. Feel his cum stream inside of me in a steady flow of heat and I grip his hand tighter, cry out his name. In this moment, the best thing I've ever heard in my life is Michael calling my name out in answer.

*I was a fool to think I could ever give him up.*

## 22

# BEAST

I stretch, feeling completely relaxed. I had forgotten what sleeping next to Hayden was like—well at least sleeping after being inside of her. I took her again last night, but I tried my best to be gentle. I tried not to hurt her. She promised I didn't, but I'm worried I should have held off that second time. It's just her body is so goddamn soft and she's so responsive. Fuck, she was still half asleep when I took her that last time. I don't know if she remembers it. I can't even be sure she'll remember the way she kissed the scars along the side of my face afterwards, or told me she loved me. *She may not remember, but I will never forget.*

I look over to find her still sleeping. Her hair is fanned out against the white pillow and in sleep her face looks innocent like a small child's. I can't resist bending down to kiss her forehead. I don't want to wake her, but I'm starved. I slide off the bed as quietly as I can. She mumbles a little in her sleep, but doesn't wake. I adjust the sheet on Hayden's sleeping body, and then leave her. I pull the door together and use the guest bathroom to clean up. I need a shower, but I don't want to wash Hayden off my body yet. I want her scent on me for a little while longer. Then I go into the kitchen. If that fucking Stroker can cook for

Hayden, I can damn well manage to fix breakfast. *How hard could it be?*

IT'S ONLY A FUCKING HOUR AND A HALF LATER THAT I REALIZE how stupid my words were. An hour and a half, a dozen ruined eggs, and two packs of burnt bacon, later I walk back into the bedroom feeling like an idiot. Hayden is awake, she's showered and dressed in a blue slip dress. She looks beautiful, but I don't like that she washed me off her body. I'll have to fix that soon.

"What's this?" she asks, when I walk in. She's wearing a smile, but I'm sure I see worry etched on her face. I need to work on getting rid of that. She still doesn't trust me completely and who can blame her after what I put her through. But, since getting her back in my life, the anger has softened. I can find a way to survive this life as long as she's with me. *I have to.*

I put the tray down on the bed beside her. "Breakfast," I tell her, disgusted with myself that I couldn't manage to fix breakfast for her. She looks down at the white paper bag with a raised eyebrow.

"You went out?" she asks, pulling the Styrofoam containers from the bag.

"The dairy bar down the street delivers. I was going to serve you breakfast in bed, but I guess since you're awake..."

"How about we have it at the table and I pour us some orange juice?"

"Milk, I want milk. There are blueberry muffins in the kitchen," I agree, helping her up and taking the bag from her.

"Saw those did you?"

"Ate two of them," I tell her and get rewarded with her laughter.

"I forgot how much you liked those. I'll make a new batch before going into the bakery this evening."

"Your muffins could bring a man to his knees, Beauty."

"Just what every girl wants to hear," she jokes.

"I think we've already seen that you have other things that bring me to my knees," I tell her and enjoy watching the embarrassment tint her face. I like it almost as much as I like watching her ass move against that dress as I follow her into the kitchen.

## 23

# HAYDEN

I'm feeling ungrateful. Don't get me wrong. Eating breakfast with Michael after a wonderful night of being in his arms, of being close to him again—is amazing. Except, in my head, I was hoping for more. Last night it felt like we had broken through walls. I thought this morning that everything would be different. Michael said he loved everything about me in the heat of the moment. Did he mean it? In my heart, I was hoping to hear him say...I love you—*not everything about me*...just... I sigh, stopping my morose thoughts.

It feels like nothing has changed. I woke up alone, not in Michael's arms, and that seems to be a reoccurring theme in my life. I hate that I expected more from Michael than what he's giving. I hate that I'm not satisfied with how great this is right now.

"You okay, Beauty?" he asks, and the simple question, along with the concern on his face, only intensifies my guilt.

"Just enjoying my eggs and bacon. You didn't have to do this, you know. I had eggs and bacon here I could have—"

"You had," he mutters, before taking another bite of his own food.

"Huh?"

"I burned them."

"But I had..."

"A lot. Yeah, I know. We'll have to go to the store. Beauty I hate to break it to you, but I don't think I can cook." He looks so disgusted with himself, that I can't stop laughing. "I don't think it's that funny," he says his voice gruff. I do my best to contain my amusement.

"Michael, it's sweet that you tried, but really—"

"It shouldn't be that damn hard. Fuck, if Stroker can cook, I should be able to, too. But damn it those eggs were defective, Hayden." I laugh again, because really, his outrage is hilarious. "I'm not lying! All I had to do was touch one of them, and it crumbled. Most of the time I couldn't even get the damn things into the pan and if I did...hell, there was so many fucking shells that I had to throw it all out. And the bacon...*Jesus H. Christ*..." *That's it!* My laughter takes over to the point I have tears running down my face and I can't even pretend to sympathize anymore. When Michael grunts at me and gives me an insulted look, I laugh even harder. "You need spanked more often," he grumbles.

"We can discuss that later if you want," I tell him, before I can stop myself.

"We sure as hell will," he answers immediately. This time he's the one wearing the smirk. I can feel my cheeks heat and decide it's time to divert the conversation.

"Why do you want to cook like Clive anyway?"

"Because he cooked for you," he grumbles again, refusing to look me in the eye.

"So?" And I think I know what he's getting at, but I'm not sure. I want him to admit it.

"When you think about a man taking care of you, Hayden— that man should be me," he answers, managing somehow to make all those words sound like one long grunt. My heart stutters.

"Michael, you do take care of me. You did last night. You're the only man I ever want to take care of me."

"I'm not just talking about sex, Hayden."

I smile. I can't help it. It's not him saying, I love you—but it's close. I reach over and grab his hand, I let my finger move over the indention of the scar. "I was too, Michael," I tell him honestly.

"I'm sorry I pushed you away, Hayden. I'm sorry I hurt you. I want to make it up to you."

*Finally!* Will this be the moment he says he loves me? My heartbeat quickens. I need to hear that from him.

"Michael, I'd like to—"

"What was that?"

"What?" I ask confused at seeing the concern on his face.

"Didn't you hear that voice?"

"Huh? Michael are you okay?"

"Do you smell that?" he asks, and I inhale. At first I don't notice anything. Then beneath the lingering smell of burned bacon and takeout, I smell it. *Strawberries.* I smelled that before. That day in the shop when the gunman came in.

"What is that?" I ask confused.

Michael looks around not answering me. Then he yells, "Get down Hayden!"

"What are you talking about? I am down," I tell him, wondering if there's something more wrong with him than I knew. I'm sitting down at the table, and he can clearly see that. Before I can question him further, he stands up and rushes toward me. I hear the window behind me shatter just as Michael gets to me. He bends over completely covering me. He tucks my head into his chest. My heart is in my throat. I hear more glass break and then I feel Michael's body jerk.

"Michael, what's going on?" I cry, my words muffled against him.

"I need you to move with me and get under the table. I want you to stay there until I get back," he tells me, and he's already moving me where he wants me.

"What's going on?" I ask, afraid I already know. A sick feeling hits my stomach. We're being shot at. *Is it Blade?*

"I'm going to find out Beauty, but I need you to stay here. Promise me," he tells me and I nod my head yes, because there's nothing else I can do.

"Be careful," I whisper when he goes to leave. He doesn't answer, because he's already running out the door. I'm left cowering under the table, feeling physically ill.

*Please be okay, I silently pray. Please.*

## ❦ 24 ❧

## BEAST

My shoulder stings like hell. I reach behind me as I leave the kitchen, finding a large piece of glass that's lodged there. I yank it out with a growl. Someone fucking shot at Hayden. If I hadn't got her down when I did it would have hit her. *What the fuck is going on?* Blade is a stupid fucker, sure. He's an idiot. I don't see him trying to kill her, though. Not with the baby still inside of her. At least, I didn't think he would. Jesus. Maybe he's more of a sick, twisted fuck than I gave him credit for.

The shot came from the right of the house. I lock the kitchen door, hopefully leaving Hayden safe inside. I didn't want to leave her, but I can't keep us there like sitting ducks either. I pull my gun out that I grabbed from the holster I had lying on the kitchen counter. I take off the safety and begin walking around the side of the house. Just as I hit the corner of the house—turning slowly so I can surprise whoever the fuck it is—I hear a vehicle start up. I stop trying to be slow now. I take off running.

I see the back end of a fucking pickup and it's fishtailing, trying to get away. I shoot, through the back windshield, trying to kill the motherfucker. The glass shatters, but the shot goes wide. I then try to shoot the tires, the back one blows and I know a moment of victory. The asshole doesn't stop, however. He just lays on the gas, ignoring the pieces of tire that tear away from the rim and spit out in all different directions. I run as fast as I can, but ever since the explosion, running is not one something I do easily. My leg has lost muscle mass and the scarring causes tightness and loss of feeling. I'm left standing in the middle of the street, staring at the truck. It's swerving like crazy and barely misses several other cars on the street. Sparks are flying from the rim which is now serving as the tire. I jog, because by this time the pain is causing me to hop, to my truck.

I start it up, and I'm backing out of the driveway, when I hear that voice again. The same voice that told me when Hayden was in trouble the other day, and the same voice that told me to get Hayden away from the window today.

*"Hayden needs you."*

The voice is as clear as a sunny day. I hear it as if the person saying it is right beside me—only no one is there. Fear makes my blood run cold. *Am I losing it? After all these years have I finally cracked?* After years of not caring what happened to me, suddenly it matters a hell of a lot. I have Hayden now. I have a new reason to keep going. I can't be going insane now. I can't give in.

For that reason, I ignore the words. I continue backing onto the street. I chance a look over at the house and guilt hits me. The voice hasn't been wrong. Am I risking Hayden's life by ignoring it now?

"Motherfucker!" I growl, watching as the taillights from the truck I'm chasing completely disappear in front of me. I slam my hands up against the steering wheel, fighting rage and the need to pursue the fucker who tried to take Hayden from me.

*"Hayden needs you."* I hear again, and I want to scream. I'm about to scream like a madman at the voice and tell it to go away. I'm driven by the fear of actually losing my mind. Then, I hear it again and this time the words take away my breath. *"Please Daddy. Go to her."*

Oh fuck. Oh fuck. *Oh fuck.*

A cold sweat breaks out over my body and I begin shaking. I've lost it. I've completely fallen apart. That soft voice. That beautiful soft voice...that can't be her...*It can't be Annabelle.* Tears sting my eyes and I try to hold them in, I really do try. Maybe I would have succeeded I'm not sure. It's then I feel the warmth. It starts at the base of my back and spreads up, reaching around over my stomach and to my chest. My heart feels so full and warm I think it might burst. And I can literally feel arms go around my neck as the heat continues to spread through me.

"Ann...Annabelle?" I whisper, afraid to breathe, afraid to hope and scared I'm right—terrified I'm not. The scent of strawberries surrounds me. It clicks into place. Her shampoo. She loved strawberry...

The voice isn't loud. It's faint and she...*it* sounds tired. I press the gas and move the truck back into the driveway at Hayden's. I don't know what to think. I don't know what I'm doing. I'm so confused. I recognize I'm crying when I have to wipe the tears out of my eyes to see to park the truck.

"Annabelle? Can you hear me? Can you talk to Daddy?" I ask her, needing to continue the connection in case...

*In case I'm talking to my dead daughter?* How fucked up is that? It doesn't matter, there's just silence. I should have kept going. Now, whoever it was that shot at Hayden, is still out there.

I unlock the door and open it roughly, pissed at myself, at the man who shot Hayden, at...*the world.* It doesn't help that when I open it Hayden is standing by the table and phone.

"Michael!" she cries.

"I thought I told you to stay under the table till I got back?" I growl, pissed off about what's going on in my head and pissed off that Hayden can't do the one thing I asked.

"Michael we've got a problem," she says again, her face white.

"Yeah. You've got someone taking pot shots through your window. That's why it would be good if you would stay where I tell you to fucking stay," I bark, shoving my hand through my hair so frustrated I can't see straight.

"Not that."

"I think that's our biggest problem right now. If you don't mind, I need to call the police—for the good it will do—and then I'm going to call Victor."

I walk over to the phone hanging on the wall, pick up the cordless handset that's resting in the base's cradle and start to dial 911. If ever there was an emergency, this would be it.

"Will you listen to me, Michael! We have a problem!"

"Hayden I really—"

"Damn it, Michael! My water broke!"

It's then I notice the front of her dress, below her waist is completely wet.

*Motherfucker.*

## ❧ 25 ❧

# HAYDEN

"Looks like you're about to deliver that baby a little early, Hayden," Dr. Mullins announces, after conferring with the nurse. "How are you feeling?"

"Nervous. But I'm okay."

"You're getting the epidural right? The nurse will be in to give that to you. Once the contractions get a little closer together, it will be show time."

"And you're sure everything is okay?" I ask him nervously, rubbing my stomach. "Her heart beat keeps dropping down lower than it has been and—"

"The baby is perfectly fine—just getting ready to meet its Mama."

His words reassure me some. I'm still a nervous wreck. Michael is by my side, but he seems shook up—and I don't think it has to do with the baby. Maybe it's because we were shot at. He took a minute to call Victor and then the cops when we first got here. He had to go out in the hall and talk to them. I thought they would have to speak to me, but apparently Michael handled it so I wouldn't have to. He came back and he's been standing by my side, holding my hand ever since. Yet, sometimes when I look up at him, his face is clouded with confusion. A part of me is scared he's about to lash out, or maybe leave. I'm praying I'm wrong. I really need him here.

"I'll be back in a bit. We still have a little while to go. I'm afraid your friend will have to leave while the anesthesiologist gives you the epidural. He can come back and visit before the actual delivery though."

"I'm not leaving, period. They can do whatever they need to do while I'm here," Michael replies, and his tone is solid, matter-of-fact and feels as immovable as a mountain. Somehow that helps me breathe a little easier.

"I'm sorry, but we normally only allow the parents or a person that Ms. Graham pre—"

"I want Michael with me. He uh...."

"I'm the baby's father," he growls. His fingers flex in my hand and my heart speeds up. I know the vow he made me that night in North Carolina, but so much has happened. I thought maybe he had changed his mind.

"Oh, I'm sorry. From talking with Ms. Graham, I understood that she and the father were estranged and that he wanted nothing to do with the child," the doctor says, looking at Michael with a hardness in his eyes.

"You thought wrong."

"Michael stays," I answer and that's the only words I can get out, but it's enough. I know by the way Michael's hand tightens on mine. My thumb moves across that groove on his hand and I try to breathe through the emotion I feel inside.

"Well that's great. Always good to see. I'll just send them in," the doctor says, relaxing. He shakes Michael's hand and tries to reassure me and then he's gone.

I look up at Michael's face and try to smile. His face is tight, like it has been since he came back from chasing the gunman, but he looks down at me and kisses my forehead. His lips move to the shell of my ear and his warm breath sends shivers of awareness through my body. How that's possible when I'm having contractions and about to give birth, I don't know—but it is...*At least with Michael.*

"We got this Beauty and before you know it, we'll be holding Maggie in our arms," he murmurs into my ear.

I'm stupid. I know I am. I was hoping he was going to tell me he loved me. It's a foolish dream and one that refuses to die. Still. Michael's here, and he wants me and Maggie in his life. That should be enough. That makes me happy.

"You're sure, Michael?" I ask him, giving him one last out.

"Stop asking, Hayden. I followed you through how many states? You're not getting rid of me. I told you months ago. I'm Maggie's Daddy now and I'm the only man you're going to let between those legs—ever."

"You're so romantic," I half laugh, needing to fight the nerves that rise inside of me. It's not flowery proposals, or confessions of love. It's still more than I ever thought I'd get in life and it's with a man I love. I'll love him so much it will be enough for both of us. Maggie will have a safe home filled with love. I'll make sure both her and Michael never doubt they are loved. It's enough.

*It has to be enough.*

## ✺ 26 ✺

# BEAST

"Okay Hayden, I'm going to need you to push with this next contraction. You're close. I need you to bear down and not stop until the contraction ends. Can you do that for me?" the doctor asks.

Jesus. *Fuck*. How long does delivering a baby take? It was never like this with Jan. But then, with Jan, I wasn't there. I was in the waiting room with my brothers. She didn't want me with her and I was okay with that. We didn't exactly like each other. Hayden is different. This is slowly killing me. I can't stand to see her in pain, and we've been going at this for motherfucking hours. She's so tired, I can see it written all over her.

"I'll try," she gasps out. "I feel it."

"Push, Hayden. Push!" the doctor urges. I support her back and she squeezes my hand tightly. I feel so fucking useless.

"You got this, Hayden. I know you can do it, sweetheart. Push hard," I encourage her, feeling completely lost.

"I'm trying!" she cries, ending the word in a growl that is so loud it hurts my ears. The contraction subsides and she sits back.

"I know you are Beauty, I know you are," I tell her kissing her head.

"Good job, Hayden. Your baby is crowning. This next contraction push."

"Oh God, I don't know if I can do this," she whispers guiltily.

"You can. You're going to push and then we're going to hold Maggie in our arms and we're going to give her everything good in this world," I murmur close to her. Her hand flexes in mine. She's yet to let go of me and I like that...Fuck no...I *love* that.

"I'm so tired Michael. Oh God, it's coming again."

"Push, Hayden!" the doctor orders.

"Michael," she whispers frantically.

"I'm right here, Beauty. I'm right here. Push out our little girl. You can do this. You're the strongest woman I know," I urge her again, and I'm not lying. She is. *She absolutely is.* Her hand bites into mine, she pulls herself up by it and immediately I hold her back. Her fingernails dig into the skin so tight I have to wonder if she draws blood.

She pushes so hard I shake, because I know the pain has to be intense, and there's not a damn thing I can do about it. She screams out my name. *Mine.* She screams out my name as she brings Maggie into this world. The reality of that weighs down on me and it pushes deep inside of me, into the dark spots of my soul that have been scarred and eaten up with hate and misery. We hear the baby crying and I slowly let Hayden fall back against the pillows. She's crying and I do my best to kiss her forehead and praise her. She's amazing.

"You want to cut the cord, Daddy?" the doctor asks unexpectedly. It feels like someone slapped me. I look at Hayden and she's crying through her tears, but she's smiling.

"*Our* daughter needs you now, Michael," she whispers and Jesus. *Fucking hell.* I'm turning into a weepy old woman, because I feel tears in my eyes. I squeeze her hand and then go over to the doctor. The nurse helps and holds the cord while I take the silver scissors she hands me and cut the cord. I look down at the baby and all I see is perfection. A dark thatch of hair crowns the perfect head, but that's not what catches my eye the most.

"How is she, Michael? Is she beautiful?" Hayden asks, anxiously and before I can answer I have to clear my throat.

"Beautiful, sweetheart. There's just...well there's one problem," I tell her walking back to her as the nurses bring the child on the other side of Hayden. One releases Hayden's gown, revealing her breasts to the world. I grunt in displeasure, despite the doctor seeing so much of my woman, I'm not crazy it keeps happening. The other nurse lays the baby against Hayden's chest.

"We'll clean her up in a second. The doctor likes to let the mom and baby connect skin to skin for a minute as long as the child is doing good.

"Oh my God!" Hayden explains, big sloppy tears falling from those beautiful gray eyes. "She's perfect, Michael! She's beautiful" Hayden cries, her hand going slowly over the baby's head.

"She is," I agree quietly, choked with emotion. She has no idea I'm talking about her. I don't know how to articulate it. I just know Hayden is without a doubt the single most beautiful woman on the face of the earth. *Inside and out.* "There's just one problem," I reiterate. The nurse comes to claim the baby for evaluating and cleaning. Hayden's eyes follow them, so I clear my throat. "Hayden, honey. We have a problem."

"What? What's wrong?"

"You're going to need to pick a new name."

"Why's that?" she asks, confused and I can't believe she hasn't noticed yet.

"She's a he, sweetheart. We have a baby boy," I tell her with a smile and the grin only gets bigger when Hayden's mouth drops open. She looks at me and then back at where the nurses are working on the baby.

"And a damn fine baby boy at that, Ms. Graham," the doctor interrupts. "We knew for a while, but you kept insisting you didn't want to know, and well..." he shrugs. "But he's healthy and the nurses will have him cleaned up and give him back to you soon. I have another delivery, but I'll be back to check on you," he says and I'm busy arranging Hayden's gown back on her to cover her up. *Fucking nurses just left her like that.*

"Oh! One more question," the doctor adds, standing by the door. "What name do the nurses put on the information for him? They'll confirm the birth certificate information with you later."

I look down at Hayden, wondering what she will tell him. She's not even looking at the doctor and she's still crying, but her eyes are on me.

"Connor Michael Jameson," she whispers. *Fuck me!* This woman unmans me. Time and time again, she completely *unmans* me. If there are tears sliding down my face, I don't give a fuck. I walk over to my woman and I take her mouth. I take it hard. I take it fast, and I take it with meaning. I take it because it's mine.

*She's mine.*

# 27

# HAYDEN

"**M**ichael? Why are there men I don't know surrounding the house?" I ask, frustrated. There's at least three guys...*three scary looking guys*, standing around my house. None of them look familiar.

"Protection. I'm not taking any chances on something happening to you and the baby. I can't be awake 24/7 and I can't be everywhere. This helps," he explains patiently, his hand at my back as he helps me up the steps. I'm holding the baby. We both had to stay in the hospital a little longer. He had jaundice and had to stay longer and I wasn't about to leave him. Now he's got the all clear and we're home—finally. He will still have to go back for some bloodwork, to make sure his levels keep going down.

"But...*Who* are they? I've never seen them before. Where's Clive?"

"Will you forget about Clive," Michael growls. "Jesus, woman. He's gone."

"Are you jealous?" I ask giggling, because obviously he is. I'd be a liar if I didn't say that it didn't make me feel good.

"Hayden," he growls and I giggle harder.

"Fine. Whatever. Who are these people?" I ask him, when I finally get control of myself.

"Can't we get Junior in the house first? So he doesn't catch a chill?"

"It's eighty degrees out here, Michael."

"Are you always going to argue with me?" he grumbles, but his eyes are crinkling, which means he's happy.

"Probably," I giggle as he opens the door to my kitchen and lets us in.

"Let me just get Michael changed and we'll—"

"We'll do nothing, Hayden. You're going to rest."

"But I'm hungry and no offense, Michael you have many skills, but cooking is definitely not one of them," I rebuff him gently.

"I can make a mean bologna sandwich."

I curl my nose and shake my head. "Um...no. No bologna."

"Fine, I bought you some tuna, I'll make you that. You whined while you were pregnant that you had to give it up," he says and he has no idea how much he has floored me. He remembered I liked tuna. He remembered that I hated giving it up. More importantly, he went out and bought it for me. I don't know where he found the time. He barely left me alone and yet, he managed to have our home protected, and make sure we had food in the house. I hadn't even bought the baby a car seat yet, but he showed up today with a brand new one. The baby loves it, though instead of leaving him in it, I'm carrying him now. I'm not supposed to lift a lot yet, so I was afraid to chance carrying him and the seat.

"I think I love you Michael Jameson," I tell him, reaching up on my tiptoes to kiss him. He takes my kiss and it might have gone further, but the baby picks that moment to cry out. We break apart and I give the baby some attention, quieting him down.

"Why don't you go rock him in the nursery and I'll bring your food and take over while you eat," he suggests.

"Yeah, I was right. I definitely love you," I tell him. I used to be nervous about saying it, but I've noticed something. Every time I tell Michael I love him, his eyes sparkle and he smiles. Every time.

Knowing that I love him makes him happy. Maybe if I say it enough, one day...*he might say it back.*

"Go. I'll try and fix you a sandwich without burning it," he mutters, which makes me giggle.

I walk through the hall and open the door to the nursery. When I got here I began drawing the images on the wall to match the old nursery. Yet, I hadn't been able to replace all the things Michael purchased. I looked and looked around here and on the internet, but I hadn't been able to find the animals again. I went with the solid color yellow to match, because I had no choice. When I walk into the room, everything is changed. Everything including the furniture. All the things that Michael bought me in North Carolina, are now here. Here in this house. Little Michael now has the nursery I always intended to give him—right down to this beautiful but silly lamp of an elephant wearing a yellow tutu.

I don't know how long I stand there, touching the lamp by the glider. It must have been a while because Michael comes in carrying a paper plate with my food and a drink. I look up at him and I do my best to broadcast all the love, and gratitude I have in my heart for him right now.

"Hayden?"

"When did you find time? How did you get it all here?" I ask him, my voice so soft that he probably has to strain to hear it.

"Victor helped me get it here, but I had already shipped it to his house after you left. I wanted Maggie...*Michael* to have it."

"Thank you Michael. Thank you so much," I tell him my heart so full it's a miracle I even get the words out.

He clears his throat out—obviously uncomfortable. He puts the food on the small shelf by the door. "It was yours," he tries to shrug off and I let it go because the last thing I want is for him to be embarrassed. "That does bring up one thing we need to discuss. You can't call me Michael and then the baby that too. It's too damn confusing."

"Do you wish I hadn't named the baby after you?"

"No...I like that he has my name—especially my last name, Hayden."

"I don't know what to do then, because I'm not calling you Beast."

"I don't want you to."

"Then what do you suggest?" I ask him, completely lost.

"I'd hate for the little guy to grow up being called Junior.

"We'll call him Connor then," I tell Michael and he smiles.

"Connor it is," he agrees and he kisses me softly. Yeah. He *definitely* likes that the baby has his name.

"Connor it is," I murmur against Michael's lips, before he pulls away. He looks down at me, his fingers curling a strand of my hair. I'm not sure he's aware of what he's doing, but he's smiling broadly and a smile on Michael's face is starting to look more and more natural.

## 28

# BEAST

"We've lost you haven't we brother?" Torch asks and inside I feel a strange mixture of guilt, regret and freedom swirl inside of me.

"I'm tired man. That life cost me everything. I'm just starting to find peace again. I can't handle that life anymore," I respond, clutching my phone tightly. I've been dreading this conversation.

"Man. Life has changed here. It's good. It won't be like—"

"But the memories will always be there, Torch," I answer him, finding that spot on my jaw, under my beard and scratching. Needing to touch it. It's become my crutch and I know how fucked up that sounds. "When I was at the club, the memories were all there. Even after we relocated, the memories followed and club life just made it worse. You guys have lives there, I don't..."

"Beast, man—"

"I'm serious. My life ended with Annabelle's. I'd walk down the hall and pass the room where she used to sleep. I'd go to my room and there were times I could smell her there. I'd hear her screams... and fuck going outside where it happened...I'd have to get drunk just to be able to do it."

"But it's different in Kentucky."

"Not really. The club is different but the memories are the same, the routines are the same. I can't live that life anymore. I just can't."

"But you're better now," he starts, but he doesn't understand. I look around the room and it's still empty. I know Hayden is getting Connor down for his nap and I'm grateful. This is something I'm not sure I'm ready for her to hear.

"Fuck man, that's just it! I'm not. Some days I feel like I'm losing it. The other day I actually thought I heard Annabelle speaking to me."

"Memories—"

"It wasn't a memory, Torch. It was...in the moment. I don't know, I can't explain it, but it felt real."

"Beast, listen man, you've been a rock through all of this. Maybe it's time to talk to a grief counselor or a therapist."

"No man. I'm not talking to some shrink about my daughter and the pain I live with. They want to act like they understand, but they don't. No one could, unless they've been through it."

"Well then, find a support group. Parents who have lost a child. Go to meetings. Reach out."

"Maybe. Someday. Hayden keeps me going. She's the reason I'm breathing. That's why I have to find the fucker who shot at her. I can't let anything happen to her, Torch. I can't be the reason another person I lo—*care* about dies."

"That's another reason to bring her here. Let us protect her. You have to know she'd be safer here, Beast."

"Fuck no. I'm not subjecting Hayden to club life again man. She's been through fucking hell. I will not do that to her."

"Jesus man. We're nothing like those fuck-heads."

"We're not, but she's not a stranger to the life either man and that's not what she wants now and it's not what she wants for Connor. It's not what *I* fucking want for Connor."

"I hear you. I do. I don't like it, but I hear you."

"And?"

"And I understand," he answers. I breathe a little easier with those words.

"Then you make Skull understand," I joke.

"Yeah, you're going to need more than me for that, dude. He's not taking it well."

"I figured," I answer resigned. I am dreading that conversation. "So any luck tracing the tags I gave you?"

"Yeah. Just like you figured, it was a stolen plate."

"Christ."

"The police found a few prints in the abandoned vehicle, but so far nothing that's raised a red flag."

"So we're no closer to finding out what's going on."

"Pretty much. Are you sure it wasn't Blade?"

"It wasn't him I chased after. I know that. I can't be sure he wasn't the one paying this guy, but something seems...off. I feel like I'm missing something. Plus...there was something about the way this guy moved. I don't think he's an amateur."

"Christ on a cracker. Do you need us to send some men down to help guard the place?"

"No. Victor's men are here. We're good."

"You know Skull's not happy about that either right."

"I figured," I tell him, rubbing the back of my neck. "I'll call Skull next week."

"I wouldn't put it off too much longer. The more he stews..."

"Yeah, I'm familiar with his temper. I'll make it soon."

"Good. It's been real, brother, but I'm going to get off of here. I got a naked woman chained to my bed and if I don't hurry back in there she's going to cuss my ass instead of giving me hers."

"Jesus! You, fucker! I don't want to hear about your sex life. I don't know why Katie puts up with you."

"I ask myself that every day. Still don't have an answer brother, but I'm damn happy she does. I'll be in touch if I find out anything new."

"Sounds good, brother. Later," I tell him.

"Later," he answers, ending the conversation.

I click my phone off and stare at it for a minute. I was hoping against hope that Torch had something new to tell me. I have to find out who's behind the attack on Hayden and I can't explain why, but something in my gut tells me it's not Blade—at least not him alone... I have to be missing something.

*I just wish I knew who or what it was...*

## ✥ 29 ✥

# HAYDEN

I just stand over Connor's crib and stare down at him. It's hard to believe I've had him home two weeks now. It seems like a dream. He's so perfect. He's turning into a greedy chunk too. He's got little rolls already started. When I was shopping for a baby, I stupidly began buying things themed towards a girl. D.D. wisely, insisted I buy some gender neutral. Still, Michael took me shopping a few days after we got home to buy more. He even picked some of it out. The outfit that Connor is wearing now, which looks like a little baseball uniform with bright green stripes running down it, is one of them. It even has this adorable matching baseball hat to go with it. Michael even surprised me by picking up a bib that said "Mommy's Little Slugger," on it. Everything in my life is perfect right now—as long as you disregard the fact that someone might be trying to kill me.

I bend down to kiss Connor gently and decide to go find Michael. He's been quiet the last few days and I know it's because he's worrying about the shooter—or at least I hope it is. I find myself worrying that he regrets being listed as Connor's legal father. I suppose there's a chance Blade might show up one day and cause trouble, but I doubt it—especially when so many people want to kill him.

As I round the corner of the hall that connects to the kitchen, I hear Michael talking. I stall my steps, not wanting to disturb him. He's the only one talking, so it has to be the telephone. I start to turn around and leave him to finish the conversation when I hear him say something that catches my attention.

I probably shouldn't, but I go to the entrance way of the kitchen and lean against it watching him. He's sitting at the table and from this angle I can see the side of his face. He's completely unguarded and that pain he keeps hidden lately is clearly there, shining like a beacon. He looks so sad that I start to go wrap my arms around him.

*"But the memories will always be there, Torch," "When I was at the club, the memories were all there. You guys have lives there, I don't... ... ...I'm serious. My life ended with Annabelle's. I'd walk down the hall and pass the room where she used to sleep. I'd go to my room and there were times I could smell her there. I'd hear her screams... and fuck, going outside where it happened...I'd have to get drunk just to be able to do it."*

His words hit me with the force of a physical blow. Michael dealt with this kind of pain inside of him for years and years. He stayed there trying to fit in and belong, all while carrying this kind of pain inside of him. How could his friends not notice? They proclaimed to be his family, couldn't they see the daily torture he was putting himself through? I can tell from the conversation that whoever he is talking to is probably trying to get him to come home. I immediately want to scream no. He's mine now, they can't have him back. I need him. *I love him.*

*"Fuck man, that's just it I'm not. Some days I feel like I'm losing it. The other day I actually thought I heard Annabelle speaking to me—It wasn't a memory, Torch. It was...in the moment. I don't know, I can't explain it, but it felt real."*

His words leave me speechless. How do I react to them? *Is that normal?* After all of the trauma that Michael has been through, maybe some of what we're going through here reminds him of his past. It would have to. Nervous butterflies hit my stomach, making me uneasy. I try to pull my thoughts away from the fear that's beginning to form. I can't judge him on this. You see things on television and read things all the time about people who have lost loved ones and get mysterious messages. *Who am I to say it's not possible?* It doesn't seem it to me, but then I've never had someone like Michael in my life. If something happened to me, I'm pretty sure I'd fight the power of Heaven and Hell just to be close to him one more time.

*"Maybe. Someday. Hayden keeps me going. She's the reason I'm breathing. That's why I have to find the fucker who shot at her. I can't let anything happen to her, Torch. I can't be the reason another person I lo—care about dies."*

I back away from the doorway and go into the living room and all but fall onto the couch. Did Michael almost admit that he *loves* me? For a second I thought he was going to say it. I grieve that he didn't...*but*, he did admit he needs me. If that's all I get, when you add that to everything else, then I have more than I dreamed possible.

"What are you doing in here, Beauty?" Michael asks from the door.

I look up to see him standing there and try to wipe my thoughts away, not wanting him to read the mild disappointment on my face, when in reality he's given me a great gift.

"Connor passed out, so I thought I'd curl up in here for a nap. Michael! What are you doing?" I cry when he stalks over to the sofa and picks me up, as if I were as light as a feather.

"Carrying my woman to our bed to nap."

"But I feel lazy if I go to bed in the middle of the day alone."

"Who says you're going to be alone?" he asks, looking down at me. I bring my hands up to tangle into his hair—he constantly wears it down now; I think because he knows I like it so much. I use my hold to pull his lips to mine. It's a brief kiss, and one of frustration because I can't have sex with Michael yet.

"In that case, hurry up," I tell him when we break apart. "This Momma's tired," I add when he smiles. His eyes brighten with joy, his smile stretches across his face, and I feel it all the way to my toes.

## ❦ 30 ❦

## BLADE

My club was never what you would call clean. We lived there. Didn't really give a fuck about much more than that. It was a place where we drank, smoked, fucked, got high, and did anything else that made life worthwhile. This place, though, makes my nose curl every-fucking-time. I hate it. Almost as much as I hate the man who owns it. Cecil "Drummer" Crayber. *My brother.* I despise the asshole. I always have. He's my older brother, who also raised me and Preacher. When we moved out we swore we'd never come back to Cecil and ask for a goddamn thing.

*Yet here I am.*

It's just another reason to hate Hayden and that ugly-fuck she's hooked herself up with. How she could let that mangled mess of flesh crawl between her legs is beyond me. Whores are all the same. Doesn't matter whose dick they get as long as they get something more out of it.

"Drummer you have to do something," I growl, tired of keeping my head down, begging like a damned dog asking for table scraps. He sits on some fucking throne-like chair in this damned office and looks at me like I'm some kind of annoyance—like I'm nothing more than a piece of chewing gum he stepped on, and is now stuck to the bottom of his shoe. Son of a fucking bitch, I'm tired of it. I get Beast taken care of and Hayden pays for the shit I've gone through, I'll show Drummer. I'll take over his fucking business. Maybe I'll let him see how much better I am at it...*before I kill him.*

"I did something. I sent my best man after Preacher's dime-bag snatch you say is responsible for his death."

"Your best man? You have got to be kidding me! He couldn't even shoot her and he had a clear fucking shot! He drove away like some frightened kid."

"You mean like the kid you hired to hold up her store? He did so much better."

"That was a mistake!"

"You seem to make a lot of those," Drummer counters and God I hate him. I lied to him when I told him that Hayden belonged to Preacher. I know if he knew she was mine, he wouldn't give a damn. He is only helping now in order to avenge Preacher's death. Not because he gives a fuck, but because he likes to send out messages that no one touches his world without dying.

It's all fucking ego with Drummer. It always has been. I look at him and I doubt I hide my hate for him very successfully. His office is the back of a meat packing warehouse. The fucking thing smells like rotted flesh and gasoline. I'm not sure why—*it just does.* There's a lone light dangling above his used desk and it's not anything more than a rope and exposed lightbulb. The only thing decent in this room is the high-backed, leather chair that he sits in. He's smoking a fucking cigar which stinks even more than the fucking room. His dark hair, so different than mine and Preacher's is oily as shit. He'd probably never get laid if it wasn't for those fucking diamonds on his hands. Money really can buy anything. If I had any left, I sure as fuck wouldn't be here.

"I did the best I could do with the money I had. It's not my fault the fucking kid messed up by getting greedy and demanding the money first," I mutter, scratching my scalp at the back of my neck and pulling my head down to get control of my nerves. I haven't had a fucking fix in days. I'm starting to suffer withdrawals. I'd ask Drummer for a hit, but the fucker would just say no. I'll find some later on the streets. *There's always a way to get it.* I've learned that, if nothing else over the past few months. That's another thing to hate Hayden for. She's the reason I've been turning tricks, and forced to take it up the ass just for a small taste of what used to flow freely in my club. *Fucking cunt.*

"You didn't tell me the bitch was pregnant. Alistair has one golden rule. He won't kill a woman who is pregnant."

"Gee, a fucking assassin with a conscience," I mock, trying to hide the way my hand shakes.

"You'd be surprised. You still haven't told me what happened to Preacher," Drummer pushes.

"You know him. He always got off on running a church and seeing how many of those sainted women he could fuck on the altar. He was going after this one and her boyfriend didn't like it when he found out she gave in," I tell him, giving him the lie with a partial truth. Preacher did love the old Reverend con, even if this time he was doing it to keep his eye on Hayden without alerting the damned Torasani's.

"I told him that shit was going to get him killed someday. He never listened to me though. Neither one of you did," the bastard says. I feel a cold sweat pop out over my body and my body jerks with the hunger I feel clawing inside of me.

"Jesus are you withdrawing? You, stupid fuck! Didn't I tell you and Preacher what happens when you mess with that shit?"

"Like you don't," I growl. "It's fine. I'll get it contained. I just need you to avenge our brother."

"I don't let that shit around me. Not now. My fucking ex was hooked on that shit. She almost destroyed my business. I was glad to see her go. Fucking cunt didn't tell me she was pregnant when she left. If she were still alive, I'd wring her neck myself,"

Drummer growls. "Get the fuck out of here and don't bother coming back. I'm not helping a stupid junkie," he orders.

He's so high and mighty. He doesn't realize I still have an ace up my sleeve. He's the only reason Preacher and I decided to take the job from the Donahues. The thought of killing his daughter and woman made Preacher and me hard for days. We fucked woman after woman after that little victory. It didn't matter that Drummer never knew—*we did*.

"What if I told you the man guarding Hayden is the one responsible for your daughter's death?" I ask him, baiting my hook and waiting to reel my brother in.

"What the fuck are you talking about? My men tracked Jan down. They said she died in a freak car explosion. A gasoline leak. My daughter was with her. It still fucking upsets me that I had a daughter I had no idea existed for years. That fucking cunt deserved worse than burning alive."

"That's where you are wrong. I did some work for the Donahue family."

"You don't do shit," he mocks.

"I did. And I happen to know they hired a hit on Beast and that the vehicle Jan was driving that night, was actually his."

"How do you know this?"

"You'd be surprised at what I know, brother. In fact, I know Beast has moved in with this bitch. Maybe you could get revenge on the man who stole your daughter from you and Preacher's ex. Want to know more?"

Drummer looks me over, and I do my best not to flinch. I'm sitting on a delicate house of cards. I have to be careful not to let them all fall down. It feels like an eternity, sitting here with Drummer staring down at me. Finally, he shifts in his seat, opens the side drawer of his old metal desk. He puts a square mirror on the table with a razor and straw, pushing it towards me. Then he takes out a small clear bag of coke and sways it back and forth, between his fingers.

"You get this, if I like what you have to say," he says, his face cold. I clamp my hands into fists to fight the urge to yank the drugs out of his hand. I better make this story good. I need those drugs almost as much as I need to see Beast and Hayden dead for the life they've cost me.

*They will pay.*

# ❧ 31 ❧

# HAYDEN

"Hayden...Hayden...Wake up..." I hear a male voice sing song. I try to open my eyes but they seem so heavy. I feel a hand tangled in my hair, slowly almost against their will, my eyes open. I expected to see Michael's face. It's not. I don't see Michael at all. In fact, I'm not in bed with Michael—which is where I was when I fell asleep. I'm in a cage...No...*the cage.* How could that be? I stood there and watched as Crusher demolished the cage. *A new cage? A new Hell?* My heart is pounding in my chest, erratically. About the only thing that is familiar to me, is that I'm in my bedroom.

"Did you really think you could get away from us, Hayden?" Blade's voice asks, demanding my attention. My eyes move to look at Blade. He's squatted down looking through the cage at me. He's drunk. I can smell the liquor on his breath. His hair is rumpled and he's got some scraggly growth started on his chin, from not shaving. His fingers are poking through the wide holes of the cage and have latched onto my hair. He gathers more and more until my head is wedged against the cage, the steel pressing into the side of my face. "Fucking bitch. You ruined everything. Did you really think I would let you keep my son from me? I'm going to make you pay now."

"Blade don't do this. Don't touch Connor. He's innocent. You don't want to hurt your own blood. Do what you want to me, but please leave Connor out of this!" I beg, fear causing my heart to thunder in my ears as it slams against my chest so hard that I can barely breathe. My body is shaking as panic floods through me. I'm losing it. I've been so good; I haven't had a panic attack in forever. Yet, right now I feel one coming on and there's nothing I can do to stop it. *He can't hurt Connor. He can't!*

"You thought you could get away with naming my son after your fucking lover? How can you let that monster crawl between your legs, Hayden? After everything you and I shared you're just going to let that thing touch you? I thought you had pride. You thought you were too good to give my brothers what they wanted, but look at you now! Willing to suck a walking freak's cock—just for protection."

"Stop it!" I scream, the panic dying down and in its place now is anger. Anger at the way he is talking about Michael—of the things he's saying about Michael. He doesn't deserve to breathe the same air as Michael. Blade will never know what it means to be a good man. He'll never be anything but scum. "Stop it! Leave Michael alone! He's worth a thousand of you! He's a good man, and he's a great father! He's everything you aren't and will never be!" I just keep screaming, all the years of pent up anger and fear are surging through me. In the back of my mind I'm trying to figure out how to get free. I have to get to Connor and save him. I need to get him away from Blade. Michael might have done that already, maybe that's why Michael is not here.

Blade pulls out a knife, and I know I've gone too far. I knew it, but I just couldn't control myself. With Blade you have to keep a level head. I needed to keep control over my emotions, but I'm so tired of people hurting Michael, of not understanding him.

I can't move because of the hold Blade has on my hair. I yank against it and feel the sting of pain, but he's not letting go. Instead, he takes the knife and slides the cold blade flat through the small opening in the cage. He lets it push against the side of my face. I do my best to keep from crying out, I have a feeling he'd like that too much and I don't want to give him the pleasure. What I need is to try and scare him, to make him leave.

"You need to go, Blade. Michael will be back soon and if he finds you here, he'll kill you."

"Really?" he snorts.

"He'll kill you. He's vowed to. You need to go while you still can."

"You have so much confidence in that scarred-up freak," he sneers.

"Michael's vowed to kill you," I tell Blade, keeping my voice completely firm. "And he's a man. A *real man*. He will keep his word! He won't stop until he does. If you were smart you would run."

"*Michael*," he jeers, "isn't going to do a goddamn thing, Hayden."

"He will! He won't stop," I tell Blade with a hundred percent certainty.

"That's where you're wrong Hayden. Beast's not going to do a fucking thing." He abruptly releases me and steps away from the cage. He's laughing and I have no idea why. He has to be even more insane than I gave him credit for. That's the only explanation. "Look at your precious, Michael," he sneers. I look frantically around the room and that's when I see him. He's lying on the floor behind where Blade had been kneeling. *Michael.* He's lying on the floor, covered in blood and he's got deep cuts all over his body. He's looking at me, but he doesn't see me. He doesn't see anything. His eyes are lifeless. He's dead. *Michael's dead.*

I'm curled in a ball because of the height of the cage, but when I see Michael like that, I fall back on my ass—*hard*, and then back quickly against the other side of the cage.

"Michael!" I scream. My world comes crashing down around me. *"Michael!"* I cry, my whole body shaking.

*What will I do without him?*

## 32

# BEAST

"Hayden! Hayden! Honey what's wrong? Wake up, Beauty. Wake up!" I tell Hayden over and over, still half asleep. I awoke to Hayden screaming out my name. Her eyes are closed and big, fat tears are streaming down her face. She's crying so hard, I'm afraid she's going to be sick. She's literally gasping for breath. I pull her into my body, gathering her up in my lap. I grasp her face with both of my hands and pull her up towards me. "Beauty, it's okay. Come back to me," I tell her, treating her as I did when she was suffering from panic attacks. This doesn't feel like a panic attack though. This feels completely different. "Beauty look at me," I order, overriding my fear and making my voice stern. I hold her face tightly, not allowing her to look away from me. Slowly her eyes open wide and she stares at me. At first I don't think she recognizes me. I don't see recognition on her face at all. Then all at once, she takes in a deep breath, so deep it's like her first breath in months. Her body goes completely still, and then jerks up as she wraps her arms around my neck. I let her, putting mine around her in return. I hold her tight, pulling her body into mine, because that seems to be what she needs the most.

"Michael!" she cries. "You're alive!" I have no idea what she means by that so I continue to hold her and stroke her hair.

"I'm here, Hayden. I'm not going anywhere," I assure her.

"You were dead and Blade was...Oh God, Michael, you were dead!" she cries again, holding onto me.

It's clear she had a bad dream and not just a normal one. It's the kind I used to have after the accident. The kind that makes you relive your hell to the point that you're sure it's real, and even after you wake up, you expect to be drawn back into it. I still have them occasionally, but not often—mostly because I rarely sleep for more than a few hours at a time. Finally, she calms down, and I hold her while she tells me about the dream. Blade needs to die. I need to make his death slow and fucking painful.

"It was just a dream, Beauty. That's all. It wasn't real. You probably just overdid it yesterday. Plus, you're worried about balancing working at the shop and being here for Connor. You just need to learn to breathe and let it go. You're not superwoman."

"It seemed so real, Michael," she sighs, curling the side of her face against my chest. She's calmer and slowly the tears are beginning to dry. I move us back down on the bed, laying down. Hayden curls around until she's looking at me. She lays her head back down on my chest, but when she immediately seeks out my hand, threading our fingers together, I smile. Her thumb moves across the scar on my hand. I think it calms her. I like that it does. It feels as if I give her something she needs, just by that simple gesture.

"I know, sweetheart. I get them from time to time. They get easier, I promise."

"You get them?"

"Night terrors? Yeah."

"Night terrors...that's what it felt like. I couldn't handle it if something happened to you, Michael—especially if it was my fault," she says and her gray eyes are so full of emotion. Before Hayden, I've never had that. That look, this emotion...all of it. The surety of knowing that if something happened to me, someone's world would be less. Until this moment, I have never had someone who made me feel like they couldn't live just as well without me. Even with Annabelle, she loved me, I was her Dad, but if something happened to me, I always knew my club would make sure she wanted for nothing. She would be happy. Right now...I'm pretty sure the words Hayden is giving me are gospel in her eyes.

"Hayden—"

"I know. I know. You don't like hearing it, but I love you Michael. If something happened to you, it would destroy me. I know I have Connor, but...may God forgive me, if you died because of me, I wouldn't want to live."

"You're talking crazy. You will always fight to live, Hayden. I demand it. Connor needs you. He needs to know that his mother would fight for him, bleed for him and he needs to always see beauty in this world, so he can appreciate it."

"I like that you say I give you beauty," she whispers and she raises her head slightly to bring her lips close to mine. "Will you stick around for another hundred years to keep reminding me that I do that for you?" she asks, her tongue darting out to moisten her lips.

"I'm not going anywhere, Hayden. That I can promise you. Those two months without you were all I could handle. The thing about having beauty in your life...Once you have something that precious and hold it in your hands, you can't let it go."

"God, I love you," she whispers. I feel those words all the way through me. She does. I see it in her eyes, I feel it in her touch. Hell, I can even hear it in her laugh.

She surprises me by getting up and moving to her knees. She pulls the cover back and swings one of her legs over my body. She's wearing a pale teal, silk night shirt. I'd rather have her naked but she still wears her bra because of the baby's milk. Still, I'd be a fool not to recognize how incredibly sexy she looks right now, arched over me her breasts barely contained by the silk bra, the lace sparkling in the early morning sunlight. My hand latches onto her ass, my fingers biting into the skin as I bring her sweet pussy against the hard edge of my cock and want to weep that she's wearing that damn piece of lace that keeps her soft, warm cunt from me.

"Fuck, Hayden, you're killing me here."

"I want you inside of me, Michael, she whimpers. I want you to fuck me," she adds, her tongue moving along my neck. I can't stand when people touch my scars. Yet when Hayden does it, it brings peace. When she runs her tongue along flesh that should be deadened and feel nothing, I swear to God, I want to throw her down and ram so fucking far inside of her she can taste me.

"Motherfucker," I groan, as my cock slips in just the right spot and she starts riding back and forth on me, stroking my cock with her body, so that the lace fabric—instead of a barrier, becomes a slick glove holding my cock softly and bathing me in heat. "Beauty we can't. You've not been cleared for sex," I remind her, just like I've reminded myself every fucking night since she had the baby. *My poor balls are blue from waiting.*

"But I'm hungry, Michael," she says, looking down at me.

I let my free hand grab her hair and I pull her mouth to mine. Our lips nip and taste each other, soft and slow at first, then picking up intensity as our hunger strengthens. Her tongue thrusts against mine as I swallow her moan of need. I grab her ass, about to forget all my self-control and plow into her when we hear it. *Crying.* We both freeze, neither speaking or moving, as if that very act will somehow put Connor back to sleep. A few seconds later the crying starts again and Hayden goes lax in my arms, her forehead pushes against mine.

"Connor's awake," I laugh.

"That kid has bad timing," Hayden mutters, flopping over on her back.

"It's dinner time. I'd be anxious too if my dinner looked that fucking good," I tell her, kissing her lips and getting off the bed.

"I'll go—"

"You lay still. I'll get him and bring him to you," I tell her reaching to the floor and putting my sweats on. Hayden's eyes are glued to me.

"It should be illegal to cover all that sexy up," she sighs.

"You're the only woman in the world who could look at the mangled scars on my body and find them sexy," I answer, shaking my head and pushing my hair out of my eyes.

"I love your scars you know that, but I must confess, I was mostly talking about your dick right now," she says playfully with a big grin.

"We're not having sex for two more weeks, Hayden Graham. Not until the doctor says it's okay."

"Whatever you say, Michael. I'll wear you down," she calls out while I'm walking down the hallway.

This is just another thing Hayden gives me. I wake up in the morning to beauty. I'm smiling when at one time in my life I never thought I'd smile again. Fuck, I'm *laughing*. When I bring Connor back to her and she fixes her bra and adjusts his mouth to her breast and I see that, I see even more beauty. When I pull her so she rests against my stomach and chest, with our baby on her breast, there's even more beauty. It's so fucking bright and large it overtakes me. This is life. This is everything. I hold them in my arms and close my eyes and enjoy the feeling of...peace.

In that moment the smell of strawberries hits the air and my heart tumbles in my chest. Annabelle is here with me too. I hope she has the same feeling of joy that I have. When the scent increases, I think maybe she does.

## 33

## HAYDEN

"I'm so tired of rain," Jenn says mournfully, staring out the window of the shop.

"I can't say that I don't agree with you. Since no one wants to get out in it to grab food," I murmur, strongly hinting.

"You're so damned needy. Can't you send your bodyguard?" she huffs.

"He's at the back entrance in the alley," I mumble, not happy with the way the cake I'm decorating is looking.

"What the heck is he doing out there?"

"Taking a piss," D.D. yells.

"He is not! He's on the phone with Victor and then he was going to call an old friend. He swears someone was at our house last night," I tell her.

"Was there?" Jenn asks, showing concern.

"I don't think so. He found some cigarette butts around the street light, but that proves nothing. Our street stays pretty busy. I think he's just being over cautious."

"Well, I'm glad he is. It's not like you haven't had way too much action lately," she murmurs.

"Amen to that. I need a break almost as much as I need food," I murmur looking up at her with a grin.

"You're really a bitch. Why can't D.D. go?"

"I'm watching the baby!" D.D. answers from the back.

"You're both bitches," Jenn grumbles.

"If that's Connor's first words I'm going to kill you," I tell her laughing.

"Fine I'll go. The usual for you guys, but what do I get that big hunk of man you're screwing?"

"We're not screwing," I sigh, "and get him the meatloaf platter, the man has a thing for meatloaf."

"I always heard it was bad if a man let his meat loaf."

D.D. groans from the back room. "That joke is older than my grandmother and she's ninety-fucking-two."

"Connor better not use the word fuck, D.D.!" I warn her.

"I'm getting out of here," Jenn grumbles.

"But money—"

"I'm using petty cash. We can figure it out later," she mutters.

I finish frosting the cake and take the pan back. D.D. is on the phone; Connor is sleeping in his bassinet. D.D. waves, and I smile taking a tray of cookies back with me to fill up the other half of the display case. I've got half of them in the case when the bell above the door goes off. I look up to see a man with long, dark, oily hair showing under a hat that he is wearing low on his head. The hat shields his eyes, but you can see enough of his face to know it is riddled with marks and small scars. Yet, where I don't notice Michael's—and Michael's are probably worse, something about this guy's is different. There's a coldness about this stranger that makes the scars look more sinister. He's also strangely familiar —though I can't see his face clearly enough to place him.

"Welcome to Charlie's can I help you?" I ask the man, pasting on my fake *"business"* face.

The stranger doesn't say anything. He looks around the room as if he's inspecting every corner of the shop. Is he seeing if it's clean enough? Since it looks like he hasn't washed his hair in a month, I find that annoying. He walks to the counter, and being this close to him, makes me wish he would leave. He puts his hands on my counter. They're covered in ink, but not the good kind like on Michael's. These are crudely drawn letters that almost look like they've been dug into the skin and then someone inked over the scars. The words aren't any better either. The right hand has "death" and "angel" is written on the left hand—one letter on each finger, all done on the knuckle. The uneasy feeling I've had since seeing him, increases. I wish I could shake the feeling that I've seen him before.

"I'm looking for a sweet treat. I am surprised your business is not filled with customers."

His words set off warning bells, but I do my best not to react. He's complimenting me, but it doesn't come off like that—*not even close.*

"We have cookies and cupcakes. I have some specialty breads. Our lemon poppy-seed seems to be a favorite." I decide to try and hurry him along so he will leave.

"I think I'll taste your cupcakes. My brother, he says your cake is the best he has ever tasted, moist and succulent," he tells me, giving me a smile that makes my skin crawl, almost as much as his words do.

"Well thank your brother for his recommendation," I tell him.

"Sad, but I can't. My brother passed away—*recently.*"

"I'm sorry to hear that. Losing a loved one is never an easy thing."

"That it is not. Especially when they die so senselessly."

"I'm sure. How did he die?" I ask, and immediately wish I hadn't.

"He was sleeping with another man's woman. I'm told the man objected."

His frank reply shocks me. It doesn't seem like information you would share with a stranger. Then again, nothing about this guy seems normal. *I really want him gone.*

"I'm sorry for your loss," I say inadequately. "Have you decided what flavor of cake you would like to try?"

"It is bad when a woman is a whore and leads a man by his dick, isn't it? She lives while my brother feeds the worms and all because she could not keep her legs closed."

*Okay this is way off. This guy is a fucking nutcase.* I also can't help but think I've seen him before—even his voice seems familiar. I'm about to call for D.D. to get Michael to come up here with me. When I hear Michael.

"Sorry, Hayden. That took longer than I thought. Skull didn't take the news that great," he says, and just the sound of his gruff voice makes things better. I turn around as the door opens.

"That's okay," I tell him, relief making my voice sound way too bright and cheerful. Michael must notice something is off because he comes straight to me, wrapping his arm around me. I lean on him for a second to calm my nerves. I turn around to face the customer, just in time to see his back and hear the bell signaling the door opening. He leaves without a word, and I don't try to stop him. I'm glad he's gone.

"You alright, Beauty?"

"I am now," I tell him honestly and go up on my tiptoes to kiss him.

*I'm always better when Michael is around.*

## 34

# HAYDEN

"Hayden," Michael groans, making me smile. I'm winning. At this point we're only four days away from getting the doctor's approval for sex. Michael has proven to be very stubborn and has resisted every attempt I've made. It probably hasn't helped that I've been giving him a steady barrage of blowjobs to help tempt him. I never meant to go all the way. I only wanted to tease him enough that he gave me what I wanted the most—him inside of me. Once I got started, however, making him lose control became a favorite pastime. The last week I've stopped—*cold turkey*. I told him he could only come inside of me from here on out. He grunted at me then, and the last two days he's downright *snarled* at me. It's not been easy, but I haven't caved —*and I really, really wanted to*. I decided tonight was it. *Enough is enough*. So, I waited until I knew he was asleep, crawled under the covers and slid his semi-hard cock into my mouth.

I didn't have long to wait. I can actually feel his cock growing in my mouth.

"Mmm..." I hum around his cock, teasing his head with my tongue.

"Fuck, woman," he groans his hands finding my hair and wrapping it around his fists. He pushes my mouth further down while thrusting his cock deeper into my throat. "You've got a mouth like a fucking vacuum cleaner," he growls, as I fight to keep from gagging. I slowly back off, and move my mouth back up his shaft. I flatten my tongue and feel the vein on the underside of his cock literally pulsate. I grin as I release him from my mouth with a loud "popping" noise. My man is not exactly a poet, he's brutally honest —gruff, but sincere. He's definitely rough around the edges. I like that a lot more than hearts and flowers, however. I trust everything Michael tells me. I know instinctively I always can—no matter how much I might not like it.

"I love the way you taste, Michael."

"God, I wish you could see yourself right now, Hayden. You're so fucking beautiful," his dark voice rumbles a second before he reaches out and clasps his hand around the back of my neck and pulls me up to him. His lips crash onto mine, wild, heated and out of control. He invades my mouth like a warrior going into battle— devouring me...*owning me.*

Before I realize what he's doing, he turns us on the bed so that now instead of sitting with my back to the foot of the bed. I'm now facing the dresser across from us. We break apart and I'm gasping for breath—the kiss was that explosive, that demanding.

"Michael," I whimper my body automatically leaning back into him, wanting more.

"Turn around," he orders gruffly. His voice is so deep it vibrates through my body, seemingly on a direct path to pussy, making me even wetter. I don't even think to deny him. I turn around, giving him my back, and thanking God that I stripped before I woke him up. His rough hands slide up my stomach methodically. They move to my sides each finger pressing into my side, as if he is memorizing every inch of my body. Slowly his hands move to my back and he pushes me until I'm forced on my hands and knees—in front of him. He moves my legs so that my ass and my pussy are open to him. I can't see what he's doing, even though I do try to look over my shoulder. It's then I look up and see him staring at me through the mirror on the dresser. "You sure you're ready?" he asks. His concern is still evident—despite the desire you can hear dripping from his dark voice. He moves his hands along the inside of my thighs, sliding through the wetness that has already pooled there. My face heats, as more of my desire flows out against his hand when he growls his approval.

"God yes. I miss you Michael. Please."

"Don't want to hurt you, Beauty," he mumbles, sounding more and more like the caveman I've accused him of being. I nearly combust when I feel his hand move up and cup my pussy. "So fucking wet. Always so fucking wet and ready," he moans. His fingers caress me, moving over my clit and through my juices, gathering them on his fingers. This time it's me who growls out in frustration when he doesn't thrust them inside of me. His hand tangles into my hair and he yanks on it hard, forcing my head up so I have to look at him through the mirror. I watch as he sucks my cum from his fingers and I'm pretty sure I have a mini orgasm.

His hand goes down and just a moment later I feel his hard, wide cock, sliding against my soaked pussy. The head teases against my sensitive skin and I thrust against him wanting him deep inside of me. He slaps my ass reprimanding me. My body jerks with the sting of pain.

"Michael," I cry out, as he brings his hand down again. I grow still—afraid to move. I feel the broad head of his dick push against the entrance of my ass. I can feel the way my cum has coated his head, but he can't mean to fuck me like that. *He's so big.* He pushes a little more, stopping before he actually goes inside. The pressure drives me crazy, but I'm afraid it will hurt. Still, I wouldn't deny him. For a second fear, relief and hunger all war with each other.

"Not yet, but soon I'm taking your ass, Hayden. I just want to make sure you're ready for me, before we do," he whispers. He leans down, placing kisses along my spine and I can't deny the disappointment that bubbles up inside of me. Michael wants me like that and I want him to use me anyway he wants. *I belong to him.* I don't worry about my own pleasure, because I know without a doubt that if Michael is in charge, he will always make sure I have nothing but pleasure. I'm about to demand he quits toying with me when I hear him murmur, "Don't let me hurt you, Beauty," he whispers and a moment later his cock is pushing inside of me.

*Finally.*

## ✿ 35 ✿

# BEAST

I deserve a fucking medal for resisting what Hayden has been doing for the last week. Jesus, the woman has practically tortured me with her body. I'm not exactly a small man though, and there's no way I could make love to her without giving her time to heal. I'm too far gone this time to call a halt to her play. We're close to her follow-up where the doctor said she could resume sexual activities if she was okay. I pray I'm not doing anything that will hurt her, because I'm too weak at this point to stop.

She arches her back so her ass is pushed up in the air. I hold onto her hips with one hand as I slowly guide my cock inside of her. I close my eyes as her hot, wet walls grips my cock.

*Perfection.*

I grit my teeth to stave off the urge to thrust deeply inside of her, letting my fingers bite into her juicy thighs. I stop with my cock half buried in her, withdraw and then carefully push him back in. It's an exercise in torture, but one that is better than the alternative—*being without her.*

"Michael, it's not enough," she cries out, frustrated. I grunt, agreeing with her, but not allowing myself to sink into her deeper

—*like I crave.* I reach my hand around to find her clit, to try and force her orgasm, without giving in.

"I'll take care of you, Beauty," I tell her, trying to reassure her that I will make sure she's happy.

"I need you more," she whimpers. "I need you deeper," she adds thrusting back into me.

My dick sinks in another couple of inches and her greedy little snatch clasps me so tightly, I can't resist. Fuck, I never pretended to be a saint. I wrap my hands around each of her thighs and pull her back into me. I keep us connected, but purposely don't allow her to take my dick any further—in fact, I raise her off of me an inch or more and we both moan out in disappointment. I lean down, letting my beard graze the side of her neck. Her body jerks in my arms, her breath coming out in a gasp. She's as close to the edge as I am.

"Stay on your knees, Hayden," I growl, my voice is so deep it's almost animalistic—which fits since she makes me feel that way. "Don't take me deep, stop when it starts to hurt. We got all the time in the world to get you used to having me inside of you again," I whisper, biting her ear and smiling when she reaches behind her and pulls my hair into her hands, knotting it around her fingers. She lowers down on my cock slowly, widening her legs on each side of me. Her ass slides against my stomach and down against my groin as she takes me deeper inside.

"Yes," she hisses, her pussy holding me tightly and coating me in her sweetness. She stops moving all at once and my body quakes beneath her—needing more. I growl, my hands move up to her breasts, pulling her back against me. I knead her tits roughly in my hands, tugging on the nipples. I don't bother trying to be gentle. I don't have that in me at this point. Her tits will carry my bruises tomorrow. *Mine.*

She's been too embarrassed to let me touch her breasts a lot, afraid the fact that she leaks milk will turn me off. *Fuck.* Nothing about her body turns me off. I get hard watching her feed Connor. I think she's even more beautiful now that she's become a mother.

She was made to nurture a child, to love them. Some women aren't
—I know that all too well. Hayden isn't one of them. Everything
about her screams love. *Every. Single. Thing.* Hell, when I feel
wetness hit my fingers, I surge my dick inside of her—sinking a
couple of inches before I stop myself.

"Sorry, Beauty, it's just...*fuck*...you feel so good," I apologize
half-heartedly. Her fingers tighten in my hair even more. The sting
of the pain moves through me and I pull against the hold, because
it feels so damn good. I kiss the inside of her neck, using my
tongue to lick up the fine beads of sweat. She tastes of sex. I move
my lips along the curve of her shoulder. I want to taste every inch
of her. When she begins riding my cock again my eyes nearly roll
back in my head. I bite into her shoulder, unable to stop myself
from marking her.

"I love having you back inside of me, Michael. It feels like it
has been forever," she moans and the sound seems to vibrate in my
dick. Before I can stop her she slides all the way down on me,
taking me completely inside of her.

"Fuck, Hayden you aren't supposed to—" I move my hands to
her hips, holding her with bruising force, preparing to lift her off
of me. I can't hurt her; I couldn't bear it if I did.

"It feels good, Michael. God, it feels so good," she whimpers.
She grinds down on me, rotating her hips, and *Jesus Christ!* I could
come from this alone—and I almost do. "I love having your cock
inside of me. I've been dreaming of you fucking me and then I'd
wake up and feel so empty," she moans and that's it. I can't take
anymore. I wrap my hand against her neck, pull her face to the
side, and fucking take her mouth while she grinds against my cock,
riding the hell out of me. I pull away biting on her lip, sucking on
it to prolong the pleasure.

"Touch your clit, Hayden, play with that pussy while you're
riding me," I order her. I can tell the exact moment she does as I
order, because her head goes back, jerking away from me. She rests
it against my shoulder, her hair trickling down across my back as
her hands go back to pulling on mine. I hold her hips and grind her

down hard on my cock—all thoughts of being gentle gone. I feel her detonate a second before I go over the edge, emptying stream after stream of cum inside of her.

"I love you, Michael," she cries. "I love you."

I have the strangest urge to tell her I love her too...

## 36

### HAYDEN

"Michael it's kind of hard to decorate cakes like this," I laugh when I feel his arms go around me. When he starts kissing the inside of my neck I give up all pretense of working.

"How am I supposed to resist?" he laughs. *He laughs.* He moves away from my neck and brings my hand up. I look over my shoulder at him and watch as he takes my spatula licking the buttercream icing off of it. "Two of my favorite sweets," he smiles.

"I was using that," I grumble. I was going to take the spatula away, but I stop. Because in that moment, my heart turns over. Michael looks completely at ease, completely unaffected by the world. *He looks happy.* His eyes are literally smiling down at me, sparkling with happiness and even with traces of pale green, glitter sprinkles, buttercream icing clinging to his beard—or maybe because of it, he makes my knees go completely weak.

"What?" he asks, picking up that I've gone completely still. Does he realize I'm staring at him like a lovesick fool? "Beauty?"

"I love you so much," I whisper, feeling overwhelmed by the emotion in that moment. This is the first time that I've got a glimpse of what Michael would have been like before Jan destroyed him and before life chewed him up—before he lost Annabelle. How can your heart be filled with love and break with sadness at the same time? I wish I could go back in time and save Michael from all of the pain that he has endured. I wish I could save that sweet, beautiful girl and give her more time with her daddy. I wish I could have loved him first. I wish I could have loved him longer so that I could have protected him...

He tosses the spatula carelessly onto the table, turning me into his arms. "Christ woman, you leave me defenseless," he growls, taking my mouth ruthlessly. The taste of buttercream, sex and Michael hit me all at once and I whimper at the deliciousness of it. My tongue dances along with his. His hands push into my ass while he lifts me up his body. I wrap my legs around him, holding onto him for dear life, and more than willing to go wherever he takes me. I can feel us moving and realize he's walking us toward the door. He pushes me up against it, using it as leverage when he moves his hand under my shirt. The feel of his rough fingers against my softer skin sends chills through me. He pushes my bra out of the way and I know where this is going to end—

*And then Connor's cry can be heard over the baby monitor.*

Michael's hand freezes. He slowly pulls away from the kiss. His head rests against mine as we both drag much needed air into our lungs. "Connor has bad timing."

"Very," I whisper on a broken giggle. We wait and Connor is quiet. We can hear him cooing and making baby noises. He's awake, but content.

"Hayden," Michael quietly says my name, and there's emotion in it. I hear it. There's so much emotion, I close my eyes and drink it in. His hand moves to the side of my neck, cupping it and using his hold to raise my eyes to him. "Look at me, Beauty," he prompts. For some reason nerves hit me. I bring my hand up to rest against his, my thumb moving against his scar. I slowly open my eyes to look at him. The emotion shining in his dark eyes makes the breath literally stall painfully in my chest.

"Michael," I murmur. *Can he hear the fear in my voice?*

"I'm broken Hayden," he whispers and guilt is heavy in his gruff words. Tears sting my eyes and I tighten my hold on his hand, my thumb pushing into his scars.

"I know," I whisper sadly, because I'd give anything to heal him, but I'm not stupid. I know that's not possible.

"I might never be able to...be...*whole.*" He gives me those words with so much force he closes his eyes. I let mine close too, feeling his pain, and letting it blanket me. I mentally will my love into him. It's useless I know, but I hope he can feel me even with the ruined pieces swimming inside of him, leaving him to bleed where I can't see or heal.

"I know," I repeat, feeling useless.

"You deserve better," he says, as I open my eyes to look at him. This time there is anger in his voice, and the emotions coming from him are intense, deep and feel like liquid that I'm absorbing inside of me.

"I love you," I tell him. "Without you, Michael, my world is black. There is no beauty for me. There is nothing but darkness," I tell him. I'm trying to explain in terms only he could understand.

"You have Connor," he tells me and I feel guilty. I love Connor. I'd lay down my life for him, but Michael brings me a different kind of joy, a different kind of happiness, he brings me to...life.

"So do you," I tell him, knowing that doesn't express what I want, but it's the best I can do right now—other words are beyond me.

"I don't deserve you. I may fuck things up. I can't even promise I won't hurt you again. I can promise I'm fighting like hell to not do that...to be a man you can depend on..."

"You are, Michael," I try to reassure him. Having let our past go long before now.

"I love you, Beauty," he whispers. "I know I'm not much, but I do love you." I can't hold it back. The tears fall like rain then. I cry and hold onto him tighter, never wanting to let him go. He can't know what he's given me. He has no idea that I thought I'd never get those words from him. "Don't cry, sweetheart. I don't want you to cry. I'm not good at this kind of thing, I know. I've only said the words to two people in my life."

"Just two?" I cry, burying my wet face into the crook of his neck. My body shaking with that small piece of information—because I know. *I know.*

"You and my daughter," he confirms and right there in my tears I vow to never take Michael or his love for granted.

*And to do my best to hold onto it forever.*

## 37

# BEAST

"Honey! I'm home!"

"Motherfucker," I groan, rubbing the side of my face.

"Is that anyway to talk to your best friend?" Devil asks, leaning against the side of the building.

"What the hell are you doing here?" I ask him. I wouldn't admit it, but I have kind of missed him. He grows on you—kind of like a wart.

"Gee, Sunshine, you're even nicer than I remember," he smirks and I flip him off which just makes the bastard laugh.

"Cheer up asshole. I'm only passing through. I had to come to Vegas to get some information Diesel needed. Figured since I was in the area, I'd come see how your sorry ass was doing without me," Devil responds, clapping me on the back. We shake hands and I toss one of the boxes I picked up at the post office for Hayden toward him.

"Well since you're here, might as well make yourself useful," I tell him as he catches the box and struggles with its weight.

"Fuck, what the hell are in these things?"

"I'm told they're large cans of fondant," I shrug, deciding to be nice and place three more boxes on the one he's finally situated.

"What the fuck is fondant and can it be used in sex?" he asks. I take the *one* lone box left—*which is also half the size of the others*—and close the trunk.

"No clue. Something to decorate cakes with," I tell him and just to prove I'm not a complete fucking asshole, I open the back door to the shop for him. That's when Devil finally notices I'm carrying one small box under my arm while he's struggling with the weight of his load. He stops and looks at me over the top of the cardboard.

"You're a sorry motherfucker, Sunshine," he grumbles, going in the door and I probably surprise both us by laughing out loud. "At least Hayden will kiss me for doing all this hard work for her, maybe she'll even let me taste her muffins."

Just like that the laughter is gone. *Fucking asshole.* I walk in behind him and then crowd him into the hall, shoving him against the wall. "Keep your hands off Hayden's muffins," I grumble, while the son of a bitch just laughs. I wonder how he'd laugh with my fist in his mouth.

"Where do you want these, Beauty?" I ask Hayden when we make it to the room. She's working in the backroom today, while Connor plays in his playpen—and sleeps—*which seems to be his favorite pastime at this point.*

"Put them on the worktable if you don't mind, honey. I'll unpack them and make sure the order is right as soon as I finish cutting out these cookies."

I stop where she's working, pull her chin up and grin at her. "You have flour on your nose."

She crinkles it adorably and tries to brush it clean. "I do?"

"Mmm...hmmm," I answer, kissing the spot and then taking her mouth. Her lips follow mine, as I pull away. "How are you doing?" I whisper in her ear—where only she can hear me. I watch as her face turns a bright pink. My dick jerks against my leg, stretching instantly.

"It's...a little hard to get used to," she whispers guiltily, her eyes downcast.

"Do you hate it?" I ask her, because as much as I want this, I won't push her into it.

"No! I like it. It's just...when I walk..." she trails off, I let my finger brush against the side of her face.

"Are you wet for me, Hayden?"

"Michael—"

"Answer me," I push.

"Yes. I'm wet," she answers, annoyed. Her voice isn't the whisper that it was during the rest of this conversation either.

"Well, I've got to say that I like the way this conversation is going," Devil jokes, slamming his boxes down on the table.

"Oh my God!" Hayden shrieks.

"Hey sexy," Devil says, leaning over the table, giving Hayden a look that is going to get his face smashed in.

"Fuck off," I growl, wrapping Hayden up in my arms. She's not exactly overjoyed with me at the moment, however.

"You didn't tell me you had someone with you!" she hisses. "Hi, Devil," she sighs, refusing to look either one of us in the face.

"He isn't someone. He's an idiot," I tell her, pulling her face up to look at me. "Love you, Beauty," I tell her, hoping to take some of the embarrassment from her face. I'm new at this, but I know I love it when she tells me the same. Apparently I wasn't wrong, her head raises up and the joy in her eyes is enough to rob me of breath.

"I love you."

"Fuck, I've missed a lot, haven't I?"

"Keep fucking with me and you'll be missing your teeth," I grumble and Hayden laughs, letting her head rest against my chest, holding my shirt in her hand. She turns to face Devil, while still in my arms. I hold her loosely, but in a way that definitely broadcasts who she belongs to.

"Touchy, touchy. Where's that pretty Jenn at?"

"Sorry, Devil it's her day off," Hayden laughs in a way that says she's not really sorry at all.

"What about D.D.?" I decide to prod him.

"She's a little...possessive," Devil shrugs. "You know me, ain't no pussy gonna own my dick."

"You got that right. Because before that happens your dick is going to fall off from slipping into the wrong woman," D.D. growls. Hayden looks up at me, biting her lip to keep from laughing.

"Don't you know it's not nice to eavesdrop on people?" Devil asks her.

"You're not a person, you're an asshole. Hay, I have a problem."

"You got more than one," Devil mutters, in response D.D. flips him off.

"What's up, honey?" Hayden asks, before they can fight further —which is probably a good thing.

"Rose got sick at school and I need to go pick her up, but I had the garage drop me off this morning...so..."

"You don't have a vehicle."

"Right."

"Well I can borrow Michael's truck and—"

"No way, Beauty. You are not leaving without me. We'll both take her."

"We can't do that Michael. Someone has to watch over the bakery. Mr. Banks is coming to pick up the wedding cake today."

"You're not going on your own. Devil can take D.D.—"

"Hell, no," Devil growls.

At the same time, D.D. answers even more emphatically. "Fuck, no! I'll just walk and get my car."

Hayden looks between Devil and D.D. and then back at me. "You could take her," she suggests.

"Hayden, I'm not comfortable leaving you alone."

"Michael, her little girl is sick. Think of how we'd feel if it was Connor. Besides, you aren't leaving me alone, Devil is here. He'll stay with me till you get back."

"Go man. I promise no one will touch her while you're gone,"

Devil adds in. I look at all three of them and I'm not fucking happy. I grunt and release a large breath. One look into Hayden's pleading eyes and I know I can't say no.

"Anything happens to her and I'm going to cut off your dick and you'll have to live your life as a eunuch," I warn. I almost want to call Victor's men over to help watch over Hayden, but they're at our house today. I wanted to make sure her home wasn't left unguarded while we were gone. I can't let Blade find a way in to hurt her or Connor.

"That sounds appealing," D.D. chimes in.

"Fuck off," Devil growls and D.D. flips him off yet again.

"Give us a few minutes," I growl at them, hoping they don't kill each other off while I deal with Hayden.

"Michael! What are you doing?" Hayden gasps when I wrap my arm around her tightly and pull her with me towards the back of the store.

"If you think I'm leaving you here alone with Devil while you have a plug in your ass, you're crazy," I mumble into her ear.

"Oh," she gasps, but she stops trying to resist as I pull her towards the bathroom at the back of the building.

## ❧ 38 ❧

## HAYDEN

"You're insane!" I laugh as he closes the door to the bathroom, locking it.

"You make me that way," he mumbles and he takes my mouth hard. There's nothing gentle in it. He eats at my mouth, hungrily and I love it. His hands come down to my ass, I moan as I feel his fingers bite into it. "God, I love the way you kiss, Beauty," he moans as our lips break apart and I force oxygen into my lungs.

"I love you," I respond, feeling those words all the way to the soles of my feet.

"I really want to fuck you," he groans and my pussy literally trembles at the thought.

"We can't. D.D.'s little girl is sick," I remind him—trying my best to remain sensible.

"*Jesus*. I deserve a fucking medal. Turn around," he orders. I quickly do as he tells me, wondering how I'm still standing—my legs are so shaky. "Brace yourself on the sink," he whispers, lifting my hair out of the way and kissing the back of my neck. I do as he instructs, flexing my fingers against the cold marble of the sink.

A moment later, I feel his hand slide against the inside of my thigh. I nearly jump out of my skin—not from fear, but anticipation. He brings his hand up slowly, letting his fingers glide gently, teasing me. I bite my bottom lip, rolling it inward just to keep from crying out and demanding more. He gathers my dress in his free hand easily and I'm starting to understand why he asked me to wear a dress this morning. His hand moves against my panties to cup me there. He doesn't move. He doesn't say anything for a minute. He has to feel how wet I am. My juices are coating the inside of my thighs and I know my panties are wet.

"Michael?" I ask, when I can't fight down my curiosity any further. His name ends with a gasp as his fingers press into the fabric and rub against my clit. "Oh fuck," I hiss, because somehow even through my panties he manages to hit the exact spot I need.

"Who does this pussy belong to, Hayden?" he asks. I can't answer him at first. He's moving his fingers around in small circles against my clit making me want more. *I need so much more.*

"You. You know that, Michael," I answer. He yanks the lacy material of my panties, down. I step out of them, barely able to think as the cool air hits my wet pussy.

"That's better," Michael groans. I lift my face to look into the mirror, at the exact time he brings my panties up to his face, inhaling them. Our eyes hold each other's and he slowly lowers them, letting them fall to the floor. "If we had more time I'd fuck this pussy while you had that plug in your ass. You'd let me, wouldn't you, Hayden?"

Forget just my pussy, with those words my whole body quakes.

"Yes. I'd give you anything you want," I promise him, because I would.

"Tonight, Beauty," he promises. I can't help but wish he could now. I'm about to beg him too—to hell with everything else. Then his hand moves to my now bare pussy and he pushes his fingers through my juices. He slides them back and forth, and the sounds fills the small room. I can't find it in me to be ashamed. Michael is the reason I'm so wet and he's definitely the reason I'm trying to ride his hand and pull his fingers inside of me.

He moves to my side and then adjusts my body so my legs are

farther out and I'm forced to bend deeper into the sink. He uses his foot to push my legs even further apart and I'm here at his mercy, displayed for his pleasure. Then, and only then, he thrust two fingers deep inside of me. I cry out, before I can stop myself.

"Michael!"

"Shh...you have to be quiet, Beauty, they're just outside and if you aren't careful they'll know I'm in here fucking you with my fingers," he says and he pushes my dress over my back so I'm completely exposed. "You have to be quiet," he reminds me, but he's grinning—almost as if he wants to see if he can make me be louder. I know he's right, I don't want them to hear me, so I bite down hard to keep from crying out even louder when his other hand twists the plug inside of me.

"Oh fuck," I groan, losing the battle.

"I love it when I can make you say that word, Beauty," he confesses. He withdraws the plug a little and I start to think it's over—right before he rams it back in. The whole time he's doing that, his fingers have left the inside of my pussy and are torturing my swollen clit. Over and over, he's moving against it, getting faster and faster.

"Michael I'm going to come," I warn him, feeling my orgasm starting.

"Hmmm...." He hums, giving no real answer.

I thought that would make him stop I really did. I thought he would just remove the plug. He can't want me to come in here with his friend just outside. To prove me wrong, he somehow picks up speed, moving those magical fingers faster and faster over my clit. At the same time, he's pushing the plug in and out in short but intense thrusts and pulls. They leave me feeling like I'm being fucked hard. When his hands move off of my pussy, I lose it.

"No! Please Michael! Put them back! I want to come!" I scream, and there's no way anyone in the entire store won't be able to hear me, but I don't care. Michael surprises me by dropping to his knees. He pulls me on his face, his beard tickling me, but feeling fucking amazing at the same time. He twists the plug at the same moment his tongue slides against my clit. I try to hold on I really do, but as he continues eating me out while fucking my ass there's nothing I can do but give in to all of the sensations assaulting me.

"I'm coming. Fuck, Michael.... Oh fuck I'm going to come..." I scream again and he keeps the plug in me, but stops moving it. Instead he all but lifts me further on his face.

"Ride my face, Beauty. Fucking come all over it," he growls and I grab his hair, holding his mouth to me and I ride him until I climax so intensely my body trembles for several, long minutes— even after I've finished.

My heart is thundering in my ears as I come down. Slowly I realize I'm still on his face and he's licking my pussy slowly, almost trying to calm me down. Carefully I pull away, my legs weak. My dress falls back down. I look down to see Michael grinning up at me. He holds out my panties he picked off the floor. I grab them, immediately putting them back on, as embarrassment floods my face.

"Oh god," I whisper, realizing just how much D.D. and Devil probably heard.

"Don't, Beauty," he grumbles, but he has a smile. He reaches under me, pulls my panties to the side, and then carefully removes the plug.

"Oh fuck," I hiss as he takes it away. My body feels strangely empty, because I had gotten used to having the plug inside of me. "Don't what?" I ask, trying to concentrate on anything but how empty I feel—or how much I want him to make love to me again.

"Don't feel bad for losing control. I like it. I want more of it." I can't really argue with him, so I say nothing. We spend the next few minutes washing up and securing the plug in the small black bag and hiding it under the sink. When he turns around his face is relaxed and his dark eyes are shining. *He's happy.* Something about that makes me feel like I won the lottery. "Kiss your man," he orders. I lean up on my tiptoes to give him my mouth and he gives me a quick, but intense kiss.

"Thank you, Michael," I whisper and he grunts in answer, which makes me smile. He opens the door with a sigh.

"You owe me tonight," he mumbles and I giggle. When we get outside, Devil and D.D. are there and they aren't even trying to act like they weren't listening in. *Assholes.* "Let's go," he yells at D.D. He gives me one last look over my shoulder and shoots Devil a warning look.

"I'll pay you back tonight," I assure him with a giggle. Michael grunts and then walks out with D.D. to his truck.

*God I love him.*

## ❧ 39 ❧

# BEAST

"I appreciate the ride, Michael. I hate that I had to ask. I should have waited until Jenn was working to take my car to the garage. It's just that noise was getting worse and I didn't want to get stranded somewhere on the road, especially if Rose was with me."

"It's okay. It won't take long to get you to the garage," I tell her —forcing myself to talk. It's still hard for me to talk to anyone other than Hayden.

"Still, I appreciate it. I don't mean to be trouble."

"I didn't know you had a daughter," I answer, mostly to change the subject.

"Yeah, she's my world. Her dad took a header off the face of the earth, and it's just been the two of us."

"A header?"

"Yeah he fell off the edge. Haven't heard from him since the day she was born. Hope I never do at this point. I don't have the best taste in men," she adds, looking out the window. I don't really know what to say to that shit, I'm not exactly *"Dear Abby,"* or whatever. So I don't say anything. D.D. reaches over and turns on the radio turning on some country shit that would make my dog howl

—if I had a dog. I don't. I have to wonder if Hayden would like a dog. We haven't really talked about life, but she seems to like it here in Wyoming. It's away from her past and mine. It's a peaceful town, I think it would be great for Connor. A boy needs a dog, too.

"Do you know if Hayden is allergic to dogs?" I ask D.D. Hell, maybe Hayden's talent for just blurting things out is starting to rub off on me.

"Dogs? No. At least not that I know of. Are you thinking of buying a dog?"

"Not sure, but kids should have a dog to grow up with. One to protect them."

"The garage is up ahead on the right," she says and then nods her head. "And yeah, I get it. Be careful what you get though. I got Rose a miniature pincher once and that damn thing bit her above the eye. My poor baby has a scar there now."

I pull into the garage, frowning. I shoot D.D. a look like she's fucking insane. *Do I look like the kind of man that would have a miniature anything?* Again, I remain silent. The sooner she gets out the sooner I can get back to Hayden. I know Devil will watch her closely, but I'll just feel better if I'm there.

"Here you go. Are you sure you're okay here?" I ask, not wanting to leave her stranded, but wanting to leave.

"Yeah, I called ahead, the car is done. Thanks again," she says already turning around. She slams the door before I can respond. She's fucking strange. I have to wonder what went down with her and Devil. I'll have to ask him later.

It doesn't take me long to get back to the shop and I pull around to the back of the building. A chill goes through, me as I get out and I smell strawberries in the air. One word pops in my head: *Run.* I don't know why, maybe it's a throwback from my military days, but I've always had a sixth sense when it came to danger. It is one of the things that made me good as the strong-arm of the Devil's Blaze. Those alarm bells are going off like crazy right now. I get out of the truck and the scent of strawberries is so strong it nearly brings me to my knees.

*Am I going insane or is Annabelle really with me?* I look behind me, thinking that any minute the reason I'm feeling like this will appear. Nothing happens, however. I'm about to write it off as just being paranoid. I make it about three steps away from the truck, heading inside when I feel it.

A whizzing sound loud enough I can hear it and it's followed by a stinging sensation on the back of my neck. It isn't painful, it's more unexpected and forceful. I bring my hand up to touch the spot and feel something soft touch my fingers. I pull on it. I look at the object in my hand confused. *A dart.* I sniff at the sharpened point and there's a foul odor clinging to it. I immediately feel like I've had way too much to drink. In fact, the world starts spinning. The cracked concrete I'm standing on appears to be floating— getting closer and closer to me. I shake my head trying to fight off the effects. I'm slow and my brain isn't working properly, but I know I've been drugged. I have to fight it. I need to get inside to warn Devil to protect Hayden. *I have to make sure Hayden is safe.* That's the one thought that keeps running through my mind.

I try to call out her name, because at this point I'm sure I'm not going to make it to the door, before I go down. I fall to my knees. No fucking sound will come out of my mouth. I try again, but my tongue feels heavy—my whole body does—and it's hard to get anything to function. I'm literally crawling on the ground, pulling myself by hands that are only working by sheer determination and panic that something will happen to Hayden.

"Hay...den..." I finally get the word out, but it's way too quiet. There's no way she can hear me. I look up at the security camera above the door. The image blurs and no matter how much I blink I can't seem to focus. The only thing I know for sure is the red light isn't on.

*Someone has turned it off.*

Motherfucker I have to get out of this...I have to! I groan out in pain as a large steel-toed boot connects with my ribs. I'm so fucking out of it, I can't even make my body move with the hit. Another is delivered and another. I lose count four...maybe five, connect. Fuck. It could even be more. I'm pushed over on my back and my body is even too fucking useless to fight that.

*This is how it ends. This is it.*

That's the one thought that rings over and over in my head. After years of wanting nothing more than to die, it's fucking ironic that I'm dying now, just when I finally want to live. Visions of Hayden and Connor flash through my mind. I hadn't realized it, but I had been planning a life with them. I had been looking forward to the future for the first time in...*forever.* I had been happy in a way I never had been, even when Annabelle was alive. Maybe I should feel guilt for that. But...I can't. Hayden is everything I always wanted in life and never knew existed. My heart hurts as the knowledge that I won't be here for her, to protect her...to take care of Connor...*to love them,* begins to settle deep inside of me. The knowledge brings pain that lances through me with the force of a blade that is red hot and forged with the fires of Hell itself.

"You made that entirely too easy," a dark voice says above me. I look up, squinting my eyes to try and see who it is—actually surprised it's not Blade. I can barely make out a face. I don't think I know him. I want to ask who it is, but I can't. Everything slowly fades to black. I accept that I'm probably never waking up. I finally manage to get one word out.

*"Hayden."*

## ❧ 40 ❧

# HAYDEN

"**A**re you going to tell me what happened between you and D.D.?" I ask Devil, as he finishes helping restock the front display case from the lunch rush. I should say he's stocking it while I'm sitting in the chair behind the counter, feeding Connor. He's taking a bottle even though it's not his favorite. Still, I've found pre-pumping milk for him makes my life easier during the work day. I would be lying though if I said I didn't miss breast feeding. We still do that at night before bed, though. I run my fingers through Connor's dark hair and wait for Devil to answer.

"Nothing to tell. Not really. D.D. is what I like to call, a woman on the prowl."

"A what?"

"She's a single mother and she's looking for a permanent man— that is not *me*."

"I don't get that vibe from her, but—and I don't mean any offense Devil—I think if she was on the prowl, you would be the last man she set her sights on."

"What makes you say that?"

"She had a threesome with you in the back of a shop. That's

not exactly daddy material," I tell him and I have to giggle when he looks confused as to why she wouldn't pick him.

"You're wrong," he denies, shaking his head no.

"I don't think I am," I laugh. Connor has fallen asleep and I put the bottle up on the counter, staring down at my beautiful baby.

"Women always want to be the one to reform the Devil. That's just facts. You girls love to think you have what it takes to tame the bad boys," he says and he doesn't say it cocky. In fact, he sounds rather matter-of-fact about it all.

"Odd. I don't really see you as a bad boy," I tell him honestly.

"Honey, I'm as bad as they come," he winks.

"If you say so. I just can't see it."

"Maybe you need glasses, darlin'," he jokes.

"I think you protest too much. You just haven't met the right girl yet," I tell him, slowly getting up. "I'm going to take Connor back to his playpen. Be right back," I whisper.

"Maybe I have met her, but I already know she couldn't handle me," Devil responds, having followed me into the work room.

"You were supposed to watch the front," I mumble.

"I eat pie, honey. I don't sell it," he smirks. I roll my eyes at him and do my best not to laugh. I'm pretty sure I fail.

"You're horrible. I'm going to sit back and laugh when some girl finally does catch you," I laughingly tell him as we walk back to the front. He follows me, laughing too.

"There's not one girl that you've looked at and wanted?"

"Thousands," he deadpans.

"I meant to keep," I snort out loud. *He's crazy.*

He smirks, but then something happens. He gets a faraway look in his eye and then it's almost as if he forces himself to look at me. The look is gone and his face is full of the mischief I always associate with him. He shrugs. "Ah! Ha! So there is one!"

"Nah. Not really."

"That's a yes."

"You're annoying. How does Sunshine put up with you?"

"Wow. Did you know that when you get backed into a corner that charm starts to crack?"

"Whatever," he laughs, not bothering to deny it.

"So tell me about this girl."

"Not much to tell. I saw her and I wanted her. The end."

"It ends after you get her?"

"Didn't get her. Turns out she's...not available."

"Married? You can't touch a married woman, Devil. It's not right."

"Honey, there's not much in life that I've done that could be called right. But, she's not married—*at least not to a man*."

"She likes women?"

"What? No. At least I don't think so."

"I'm afraid I'm not following then, Devil. Maybe you could dumb it down for me."

He laughs, shaking his head. "You're just what Sunshine needs in his life."

"I'm trying to be, but you need to quit changing the subject," I reprimand him.

He sits down at one of the empty customer tables with an exaggerated sigh. "What is it with women and their need to constantly bust balls?"

"What is it with men and their need to avoid serious questions?"

"Jesus. Fine. She lives in a convent."

I'll be the first to admit that I wasn't sure what he would come back with. The last thing I expected, however, was that the woman who had caught his eye lived in a convent. I open my mouth to try and say something appropriate. Then I close it, realizing there's *nothing* I could say.

"Do you smell strawberries?" I ask instead, because right then the scent hits me strongly.

"And I've left her speechless," he jokes, still looking a little uncomfortable.

"No. I'm being serious. Do you smell that?"

"I just figured it was something you had fixed to sell," he shrugs.

"No. It's so strange. You know, I smelled that same exact scent when that man tried to rob us."

"I doubt he's coming back. I think he's still in county lockup."

"Yeah. Still, it's weird right?"

"If you say so. Shouldn't it be about time for Sunshine to get back here?"

"I would have thought so. Maybe D.D.'s car is still messed up," I tell him. I take out my cellphone and try to call Michael, but it just goes to recording. "No answer. I'll try D.D.," I tell him, already dialing the number. Her phone goes straight to voicemail too. I leave a message and sigh, looking up at Devil.

"We'll give them a little more time. I'm sure it's fine."

"Yeah. You're probably right. How about I teach you how to frost cupcakes to pass the time?" I ask him, trying to ignore the warning bells going off in my head. There's no reason for them. The door opens with the chime and a couple of young girls walk in.

"Saved by the bell," Devil jokes, laughing and I try to smile with him. "Quit worrying, Hayden. Michael's a big boy. I'm sure everything is fine."

"Yeah you're right," agreeing with him as I go to help the new customers.

*I just wish I believed him.*

## ❧ 41 ❧

## HAYDEN

"I just don't understand where he could be!" I cry. I'm in my car driving around and around the area, looking for any sign of Michael. It's almost eight o'clock now and it's starting to get dark. We've been searching for over three hours— ever since D.D. called to let me know that she hadn't seen Michael since he dropped her off around two this afternoon. That means that Michael has been missing for six hours. *Six long hours.* I have D.D. watching Connor while Jenn, Devil and I are searching for Michael. I asked Devil to pick Jenn up. I figured three sets of eyes were better than two, but I'm starting to lose hope.

"Maybe he left, Hayden."

Jenn's words strike fear deep inside of me. Cold hits me. Could I be wrong about Michael? Would he have left? I don't—

"Bullshit."

"I'm just saying—" Jenn defends.

"I don't give a fuck what you're saying. I was with that man when Hayden left the first time. He was a wreck. He hauled ass after her, just to make sure she was okay, and he stood outside her home every fucking night for a month, all to keep her safe. Nothing, and I mean nothing, would make him leave of his own freewill. Not now—not ever. His whole life is Hayden and that boy."

Devil's words make my heart swell. Tears sting my eyes and I feel like I'm suffocating in fear. I close my eyes, trying to get a grip on it all, Devil reaches over and puts his hand on my shoulder, giving it a squeeze.

"Devil's right. Michael wouldn't leave me or Connor. He loves us," I tell Jenn and my heart turns over just saying the words out loud.

"Then where the hell is he?"

"Blade has him," I whisper the words Devil and I are both thinking. Devil pulls into an empty parking lot that goes to an old abandoned grocery store.

"It's starting to look that way," he says resignedly.

"What do we do? How do we find him?" It's really impossible to keep the fear out of my voice now.

"I think I need to call in the brothers. I know that might not sit well with you, Hayden...but..."

"I'm not important. If they can help him, call them. We need Michael back. We need him back *now*, Devil. *Now*," I stress, grabbing Devil's upper arm to plead with him. I'm terrified about what Blade could be doing to him, even now.

"Then let's get Connor and go back to your house and set up a command center."

"I don't want to wait. We need to—"

"Blade might contact you still. He's going to want Connor. We need to be there just in case, Hayden."

"But Connor..."

"Will be safer at home with you, where there are people guarding you both."

I swallow down my fear and nod my agreement...all while sending up a silent prayer.

*Please let Michael be okay. Please God, let him be okay.*

## 42

# BEAST

My head feels like someone is inside of it with a sledgehammer. I keep my eyes closed doing my best to piece things together. My body is sore, but everything seems to be working. My arms are above my head and from the pain coming from my wrists, I'd say I'm tied up by them. My legs are dangling, so I'm definitely off the floor. Slowly I open my eyes. The light in here is shit and it takes me a bit to make out exactly where I'm at. It's an old warehouse of some type. Everything around me is either metal or concrete and there's a stench in the room reminds me of a mixture of old piss that's been sitting for days and rats. My nose curls in revolt. I look around a little more. To be honest I'm expecting to see Blade. I'm more than a little pissed at myself that the fucker managed to get the drop on me. He's not there though. No one is. I seem to be alone.

I move my hands, experimenting to see if there's any give in the ropes. The rope is made of a harsh nylon and it's tied so tight my fingers are numb from the lack of circulation. I do my best to move my hands apart, but the rope refuses to give. I can already tell the skin beneath the rope is raw. I have to wonder how long I've been hanging like this. My tied, joined hands are being held by a giant meat hook like you'd see in a butcher's freezer—only instead of a slab of beef it's me hanging. I look around for something—anything that might help get me free. *I come up with nothing.*

"I see you are finally awake. I was beginning to wonder. I thought perhaps we had put too much of the drug into the darts. I would have hated to kill you before we met. That wouldn't have been fun at all," a man speaks up from the corner. He's hidden in the shadows and I can't make him out at all at first. Then he takes a step out and then another one. Sadly, he doesn't look a bit more familiar. I don't get it. I don't know him. Why is he holding me here? *Why did he kidnap me?*

"Who are..." I end up coughing before I can finish the words. My throat is so dry it feels like I have sand in it. "Who are you?"

"Who I am might surprise you," the man says, telling me nothing.

"So, surprise me then," I demand, frustrated. I keep trying to work my hands free, but I know it's useless.

"I will—eventually. You're going to be with me for quite a while. I can't rush this. My revenge is one I have to savor," the asshole says. My eyes are starting to focus and I can see him clearer now. He's got oily hair that falls to his shoulders. His face is ravaged by scars, though I suppose I am the last one to worry about that. His fingers are covered in rings. He has them on every one, and sometimes there are two on one finger...maybe more. He's wearing an expensive suit, though it's not really tailored well. He's nothing like the Donahue's so I can't figure out why he feels he owes me revenge.

"Listen, I think you got the wrong guy. We don't know—"

"Trust me, Mr. Jameson. I know exactly who you are and soon you will know who I am."

"Fine then just tell—"

"I will tell you, but not today. Perhaps tomorrow. Tonight I shall let you rest and anticipate all the fun we will have tomorrow."

"Listen, you sad fuck. If you want to go toe-to-toe with me then let's do this shit," I growl. It's useless though. The man ignores me, turns out the already pale light in the room and slams a heavy steel door behind him. "Fuck!" I scream. I've got to figure out how to get loose from here. I have to get back to Hayden and Connor. I need to make sure whoever this man is—he can't touch them.

*I just have no fucking idea how I'm going to do that.*

## 43

# HAYDEN

"You okay, Hayden?" Devil asks from the door of the nursery. I don't turn around and look at him. I remain looking down into the crib giving him my back. It's the next day and Michael is nowhere to be found. We've heard nothing from him—*or anyone*. No. I'm not okay. *What kind of question is that? Am I okay? Hell no. I'm slowly dying.*

"We still haven't heard from Blade. We're not even sure he's the one who has Michael. We're not sure Michael is still..."

"Hayden," Devil interjects, but I'm driven to finish it—to speak my greatest fear.

"We're not even sure Michael is still..." I stop talking as my voice breaks. I have to force myself to continue because the word is choking me and torturing me with just it's presence. "Alive," I finally finish.

"He's alive. Michael is a fucking tough bastard. He won't give up until he's back here with you," Devil argues. Maybe I should try to believe him, but I can't. I just feel...*hollow*. It all feels empty and hollow, I need Michael.

"Yeah," I tell him quietly. I just want this conversation done. I want to stand here and look at my son. Watch the way the dark curls fall on his head, see how peaceful his face looks when he sleeps and take in his beautiful baby smell...

"Diesel is coming in with five of his men. Skull and Michael's old crew are too, but they will probably be a few days behind my club."

"Why are you calling him Michael? What happened to Sunshine?" I ask, I could care less about the men showing up. He has confidence in them, but I don't. I'm not sure I have confidence in anything anymore.

"I'll be back to calling him Sunshine soon. It's no fun unless he's here to give me shit over it. I like that grunt and the look of disgust he likes to send my way," Devil answers. If my heart didn't feel like it was being ripped out of my chest, I could almost smile.

My fingers tighten on the railing of the crib as I imagine Michael looking at me with that same look and grunting. *I'd give anything in the world just to have him here, grunting at me again.*

"He did have a way with a grunt," I whisper. I close my eyes and I can almost feel his arms go around me, warming this deep chill that seems to have settled into my body. Feel his beard tickle my neck and hear his voice vibrate as he says my name. I didn't appreciate how amazing that was when I had it. I didn't take enough time to cement it in my memory. The fear that seems lodged inside of my throat right now is entirely selfish. It's not because I'm worrying about what is happening to Michael right now. It's because I'm petrified he won't make it back to me and I'll never feel him hold me again.

*I don't know if I could survive...*

"Hayden, you have to snap out of it. You have to believe that Michael is going to be okay. He'll survive this. He's going to come back to you," Devil says and he must have moved from the door because I feel his arms go around me as if to hold me. It feels wrong. *It all feels so wrong.* His touch is not sexual, it's meant to be comforting, but regardless...*it's not Michael's.*

I jerk away from him, as if his touch was acid and burns me. I turn and look at him and I hate the look on Devil's face. He's not being truthful. He might be spouting all this nonsense about Michael making it back, but he doesn't truly believe it. I see the truth in his eyes right now too. *He thinks Michael is dead.* I saw the truth in his eyes when we discovered the security camera at the bakery was disabled. I want to scream at Devil for giving up and trying to placate me. I want to demand he leave. Before I can do any of that, his phone rings. I turn away to stare at my son again. Mine and Michael's son—because that's who Connor is.

"Where?" I hear Devil say in the background. Something in his voice makes me turn around. "I'll have someone there in ten. Don't touch anything," he orders. When he hangs up I immediately ask.

"What is it?"

"Victor's men found Michael's truck," he answers, and fear and hope wage a war inside of me—*all over again.*

"Was Michael there? Where did they find it?"

"It was just the truck. There's no sign of Michael."

"Where? Can we go and see it? Maybe there's a clue in it that might help us find him. I'll get D.D. to watch over Connor. There's still one of Victor's men here, he can watch over them and we'll—"

"Hayden slow down. You need to stay here where you're safe. Michael's truck was found half-submerged at Miller's lake."

"Are they sure he wasn't..."

"He wasn't in it. My man said it looked like someone had tried to push it in and left it alone when it didn't sink in further."

"I'm going to see it," I tell him, already headed to my guest room to tell D.D. She dropped her daughter off at her mom's, and then came here to help with Connor. I told her it wasn't necessary then, but now I'm glad she did.

"Hayden—"

"I'm going, Devil," I growl over my shoulder, and in a tone Michael could be proud of.

I just hope there's something there that will give me an idea of what happened to Michael...

# 44

# BEAST

"You're not looking so good over there, Beast."

I shake my head to try and clear it. I've been here just four days...*at least I think that's how long*. The fucking asshole who comes in here to torture me daily, still hasn't told me who he is. He keeps telling me that he'll tell me when the time is right. The way he's been working, I figure the time will be right when I'm dead. I'm still hanging from a hook. The skin around my wrists have pretty much disintegrated, leaving a raw, meaty ring that is burning like fuck, either from holding my weight or from infection. I can't tell which. The bastard is enjoying torturing me. The first day I laughed at him as he turned the overhead water sprinkler on me. Who does that shit? Then he added the electricity that came from a battery and charger he had wheeled in. The current he shocked me with was small at first, though it did hurt like a bitch. The second day he increased it to the point that I thought he was going to kill me then. My body went through seizures for long agonizing minutes, even after the cables were removed. I've been hanging here, wondering how much more I could take. Three or four days might not seem like a lot, but those days are without food, water, and while getting enough volts to leave my head fucked up...

I shake myself to try and concentrate on the here and now.

"I knew you were behind this, Blade. You, cocksucker."

"You shouldn't have tried to come between me and what's mine, Beast. You had to know I'd get you...*eventually*."

"Hayden's not yours. She's never been yours. Not my fault you're too much of a pussy to accept that," I growl.

"Big talk from a man who's hanging like a slab of meat."

"Get me down from here and face me like a man," I goad him. Honestly, in the fucking shape I'm in, I'm not sure I could take him, but I sure as hell would like the chance to try.

"He can't get you down. He's not in charge," the other man says coming in through the door on the side.

I close my eyes, doing my best to try and focus. I squint them tightly and reopen them. It doesn't help much, but I can see the man walking towards Blade.

"I thought you might be half-way smart. What the fuck you doing helping out this sad fuck?" I ask him, hating that my voice is starting to sound weaker.

"A sad fact we do not pick our family."

"Family?" I ask, surprised. They remind me nothing of each other—except for the fact I want them both dead.

"He's my brother. Just like Preacher. I don't like either of them, but a man must defend his family—or else he is not a man," the guy says and I feel like he's speaking in riddles.

"Who the fuck is Preacher?" I growl, feeling a wave of nausea threatening to overcome me.

"The man you killed."

"You're going to have to be more specific. I've killed a lot of men," I respond, counting backwards in my head to fight down the urge to wretch empty air. That's all that is left when I vomit now and I won't do that in front of these fuckers. I won't give them the satisfaction.

"My brother you burned alive in my club! *You, motherfucker!*"

Blade screams charging at me. He has a knife drawn and he stabs it into me, connecting somewhere below my stomach. I can't tell where exactly. The pain is intense, but when he hit my body, I began swaying back and forth. The rope I'm dangling on jerks and the rough nylon cuts into my raw skin and that pain hurts much worse than anything else.

I fight the pain down, when it feels like I'm going to lose consciousness. I'm still swaying, but I see the other guy grab Blade by his collar and pull him back.

"What the fuck do you think you are doing, Earnest? This one is mine. He owes me. You do not touch him," the guy screams at Blade while slapping him hard across the face with the back of his hand. I figure with the amount of rings on his hand that has to fucking hurt.

"His name is Earnest? Fuck, that's rich," I grunt, wondering if it wouldn't be smarter to give into the pain and blackout at this point.

"Shut up!" Blade screams and he never had a solid foot on sanity to begin with, but he definitely seems unhinged now. "Do you see how he mocks me? He killed Preacher and let him burn inside my club! He took Hayden and the baby too! Then he kept them from me! He has to die! I need to kill him! I'm the one who needs revenge, Drummer! Beast destroyed everything I built. He took away everything!" Blade continues and I do my best to let my tired mind pick up the details.

"Jesus that fucking reverend who tried to take Hayden was your brother? You got quite the twisted family tree, *Drummer*," I tell him stressing his name, so he knows I at least have that information now.

"I will get revenge for our brother and I'll reclaim his woman and child and make them mine. This is none of your concern," Drummer says and his words chill my blood like ice. I thought I was fading, but there's no way I'm letting this asshole get his hands on Hayden or Connor. Diesel will be working on finding me. *I just need to keep him distracted.*

"Hayden and the baby are mine," I growl.

"You'll be dead soon," Drummer shrugs, "but then they weren't yours to begin with—were they?"

"They've always been mine," I argue.

"No. They belonged to my brother, Preacher, first. Do you spend your life taking women from other men? Can you not claim one of your own? Are you so weak that you have to take what another man owns?" Drummer asks, turning to look at me.

"Preacher? Is that what that ass-clown told you? Preacher never touched Hayden. Blade did. He kept her caged up like an animal until she thought he saved her by setting her free. That's the only way his ass can get a woman. He has to make himself look like a hero because he knows once they see how small his dick is, they'll run away."

"Fuck you! Hayden was mine! You and those fucking Torasani had to get involved! But I told you I'd make you pay! I'm going to make you all pay!"

"You lied to me?" Drummer screams as he turns to Blade. His hand goes around Blade's throat.

"I needed revenge!" Blade screams out, clawing at his brother's hand. Drummer pushes him all the way to the wall. Blade's body hits with a large thud.

"You lied to me about everything!" Drummer's back is to me and I can't see much of what is going on, but from the choking sounds I'm hearing, I think Blade will be dead soon. "And you conveniently left out the Torasani—*didn't you brother?*" Drummer hisses.

*Good riddance, Blade.*

"No!" Blade screams. "I didn't lie about your daughter! That was the truth! I swear! You wouldn't have helped if you had known about the Torasani and—"

His words end with a horrible gurgle. As Drummer steps away from Blade, I see him fall to the ground. His head at a weird angle. I squint to focus my vision and see that Drummer has slit Blade's throat. He didn't do it gentle either. The cut is ragged and from the blood on Drummer's hands, I'd say he finished the job up by his hand.

"We'll resume our torture session tomorrow. I've found I've killed enough for today," Drummer tells me and his tone and voice are almost normal now. It's like someone flipped a switch off, from anger to calm. *Christ.*

He turns out the light and leaves. I listen to the door slamming and wait as the sound echoes in the room. I wanted to ask Drummer exactly what Blade meant about his daughter, but I didn't, it will be something I goad him with whenever he comes back.

For now, I close my eyes, giving myself permission to rest. Just like every day since I've been here, when I close my eyes, I'm surrounded by a feeling of warmth and the fragrance of strawberries.

*Annabelle is with me.*

## ❧ 45 ❧

# HAYDEN

"You must be my boy's cariño, Hayden."

I jerk up at the voice. I look up to see an older man, probably late forties, looking down at me. He's obviously of Spanish descent. You can tell from looking at him as well as the language. His dark hair glistens. There are deep shimmers of gray thrown in and it makes him look sexier somehow. He's covered in ink, and when I say covered, I mean I can see it on his neck, his fingers, and his arms. Basically, all of his skin that's visible past his white t-shirt and his black MC cut, is ink covered. I know instantly who it is, because Michael has told me about him. I'm just surprised to see him. I thought Devil said he would take longer than Diesel to get here.

"You must be Skull," I answer, standing up. I'd been sitting in the chair by Connor's bed. Connor is sleeping, but being with him helps me to calm my nerves.

"Do not get up, querida. I do not mean to bother you. I just wanted to see you."

"Why?"

"Because you are a spot upon my conscience."

I stuff my hands into the back pockets of my jeans to keep from wringing them together. Skull's dark eyes are literally boring into me, making me uncomfortable. "I don't know what you mean."

"I should have sent men to check on you sooner. My anger at your brother...." He shrugs trailing off before finally adding, "Mi ira me cegó."

I don't remember much about high school Spanish, but I get the gist. *He let his anger get the better of him.* I'm not sure how I feel about my brother at this point. I know he betrayed me. I know I owe him nothing, and it might make me an unfeeling bitch, but I don't grieve him. I don't miss him. So, I shrug off Skull's concern now.

"My brother was an asshole."

"Si. He was, but he knew he was dying and he asked me to have someone protect you and I did not. I didn't out of anger at what he had cost me. It was wrong of me, querida. I am sorry for that."

"Is that the reason you sent Michael my way?"

"Si. Though way too late to—"

"The way I look at it is, I owe you for sending Michael into my life. Whatever else happened doesn't matter now. Not really," I tell him, unsure of how I feel, knowing my brother worried about me as he was dying. Apparently I really am cold, because it just seems too little, too late.

"On this we do not agree, querida. I feel it is I that is in your deuda."

"Can we just speak English here?" I finally ask him, frustrated. Skull laughs. I didn't expect that at all.

"You remind me much of mi cielo. My Beth. You would like her. I just meant, Hayden that I think I am in your debt."

"I don't agree, but if you bring Michael home to me, we can call it even."

His face goes serious with my words, almost grim. "I will do my best, querida. I promise you that."

I nod, and then turn back around to look at Connor, dismissing him. I can't deal with him right now. I can't deal with any of them. They don't understand. It's not their world that is on the line.

*It's mine.*

## 46

### BEAST

Two more days in hell. *I think.* Fuck, I'm not sure anymore. I have a fever. The cut that Blade gave me wasn't deep, but his knife was as fucking dirty as the rest of him. I haven't seen much of Drummer. He came in and juiced me a couple of times. He keeps talking cryptically about shit that I can't really grasp and then leaves. He's been preoccupied since he offed his brother. I'd like to say it's because he felt bad about it, but since his brother's body is over in the corner stinking—I doubt it. I close my eyes, letting my head loll back. I'm exhausted. I need to just quit fighting it. Devil will watch over Hayden and Connor. He'll make sure they're safe. *I'm just so tired.*

I'm almost out again when a familiar warmth fills my system and the scent of strawberries blossoms around me, overtaking the horrid smell of Blade.

*Hold on, Daddy. Hayden is coming.*

I hear the voice. I've heard it several times today...or maybe the last two days...I can't remember. Everything is hazy. I know logically it can't be real. The infection has probably spread to the point that I'm delirious, still the words chill me.

"No!" I scream out into the nothingness. "Hayden can't come. She can't be here! She doesn't belong here!"

"But she does. I think it would be marvelous to have her join our little party. Her and Connor. I'm working on arranging that now."

"No! You don't need to involve her. Your fight is with me. I'm the one who killed your brother. Do whatever you want to me, but leave Hayden and my son out of this," I growl, screaming the words, senselessly trying to get free. It doesn't help. I end up swaying back and forth and feel the pain of the ropes. You would have thought my hands would stop hurting after all this time. The truth is it's more painful now, because my hands are constantly numb. It's like they're persistently asleep from being locked in the upright position and holding all my weight—without a break. Because of that, the pain takes on an added depth.

"Your son. How easy you lay claim to another man's child. It is pathetic. Our fight has nothing to do with my brothers. They were idiots from the beginning. I tried my best, but their blood was tainted by their whore of a mother. My father was a lot like you, Beast. He was never choosy about where he stuck his dick."

"What is our fight about then? Tell me asshole! Just tell me already!" I growl, still fueled by panic at the idea of this monster getting his hands on Hayden or Connor.

"You took the most valuable thing a man can have from me. I plan on taking it from you. It seems only fair," he shrugs as he walks toward me. He's getting ready to send more electricity through my body. Will this be the one that kills me? On their own they're not powerful enough to achieve it, but I've been withstanding this for days. *Fucking days...maybe even a week or longer.* Can I truly stand much more? I want to say no, but every time I get close to caving, I see Hayden's face. I hear Connor's little baby noises, I feel Annabelle surround me—and I hold on.

*I once was a man who had nothing. Now, when I have everything to live for, I will most likely die.*

"You're fucking crazy. Hayden and Connor have nothing to do with whatever score you have to settle with me. They're innocent!"

Drummer attaches the cables on me and I feel the water begin to drench me. I know what's coming next. I despise it—but I feel fear. I don't know if I'm strong enough to keep surviving this, and I need to. I need to be strong for Hayden.

"Have you not figured it out yet that no one is innocent in this world?"

"Hayden is!" I growl, trying to kick out at the asshole when he gets close to me. It doesn't come as a surprise when I achieve nothing. I'm so weak, I can barely manage to move my legs.

"She might be, but Jan wasn't, was she Beast?" My blood runs cold at the name.

*Jan.*

"I see you're trying to understand. Maybe you already do, but are just refusing to admit it."

"I don't know what—"

"Let me clear it up for you," he interrupts me as he walks back to the battery charger. "Jan was mine. She was a lying cunt, but she was mine. She left me for another man. One who would put up with her lying and whoring—one who was not man enough to *punish* her."

"You're lying!" I cry out, refusing to believe him. Could all this have to do with Jan? *Hasn't she ruined my life enough?*

"Imagine my surprise, when I found out the lying bitch was pregnant with my daughter."

No, no, no, no.... *No!*

The word keeps repeating in my head. He can't be saying what it sounds like. It's a trick brought on by the infection. *It has to be.*

"Imagine my surprise," he continues, even as my mind tries to reject what he's saying. "When I found out my daughter died before I ever knew about her. You see, *Beast,* we have a lot in common. And I'm going to take what you claim as yours, just like you took from me."

He throws the charge and instantly my body begins shaking.

He doesn't leave it on long, but it feels like an eternity. He's gone mere moments later—even before I have stopped convulsing. The water goes off, but I don't notice it. The wetness from the water is pouring down my face, but it could be from tears. I'm crying. I'm crying and my body is swaying from the force of the sobs.

"No. No. No. *No.*" I just keep repeating the words over and over, until slowly I'm enveloped with the heat and the scent of strawberries. My tears fall harder, but the words change to just one. It's just one, but I cry it out in a sound so full of sorrow I couldn't explain it to another person. It's being torn from what's left of me because I'm shattered. *Completely broken.* Crying, alone in the dark and sobbing my daughter's name.

"*Annabelle.*"

## ❧ 47 ❧

## HAYDEN

"Have you found him yet?" I ask Devil. The look on his face gives me the answer. I give a scream that's pure frustration and stomp off. He follows me, but I wish he wouldn't. I feel like we've been doing nothing but twiddling our damn thumbs. Each day that passes, I begin to lose a little more hope. I know that every day that goes by is another day that Michael could be dying—*or dead*. Devil and Skull both assure me over and over that they are doing everything they can to find Michael, but from where I'm sitting it's just not working.

"Hayden! Where are you going?" Devil asks when I make it to the kitchen door. I hold my head down at the doorway and do my best to get control of my emotions.

"I'm going into work," I tell him, pulling in a deep breath.

"I don't think that's wise right now. There's too much unknown. I think it would—"

"I'll take one of Victor's goons with me, Devil. I just have to get out of here. I think if I spend one more hour inside these four walls, not knowing where Michael is or what is happening to him, I'm going to go insane. I just need...*air.*"

"Hayden."

"Please, Devil," I ask, looking over my shoulder and not bothering to disguise the anguish I feel inside. He studies me for a minute before finally agreeing.

"Luke you follow her and stay one step behind her. Don't let anything happen to her."

"Got it," I hear the man say behind me. I'm not sure which one is Luke. I don't really care. I make it to my car and put my head down on the steering wheel. That's when I let the tears fall. Not many—if I give into all of them, I'll never get out of here. I reach into the console getting a tissue and just my luck it's empty. I don't see anything around the cup holder either. I look above the visor and a folded white sheet of paper falls out and floats to my lap. I don't remember putting it there, but life has been crazy. I unfold it carefully, my heart nearly stopping at what I read.

*I've got Beast. All I want is you and Connor. If you want to keep him alive, ditch your guards and meet me out at the old clothing factory on the state line. Any sign you have company and he's dead.*

That's it. Nothing else. It has to be Blade, though I will admit the writing—while similar looks different. I want to take it straight to Devil, I start to, but then I panic. What if they all show up and the bastard kills Michael? I can't let that happen. I'm not stupid, I know if I walk in—especially without Connor—chances are Blade will kill both of us. I don't doubt that's been his plan all along. I have a big decision, but in the end, there's nothing else I can do. I wad the paper up in my hand, get out of the car and walk back to the house.

I look over my shoulder at the man that Devil has following me —Luke. "I've decided I would rather spend time with Connor," I tell him. He shrugs and then walks around the house where a couple of the other men are standing.

"I thought you were going in to work?" D.D. asks, surprised when I come in the nursery. My heart is beating in double time. I don't answer at first. The enormity of what is going on, is almost too much. I go to the cradle and pick up Connor. He places his little chubby hands against my chest as I cradle him close. I kiss the top of his head and breathe in his scent as I war with the decision I'm about to make.

"D.D. I need a favor," I whisper, almost afraid of what I'm going to say.

"What's going through that head of yours?"

"I know where Michael is." I answer shakily.

"Oh my God! That's great! You need to tell Devil and the men so they can—"

"I can't do that."

"Why in the hell can't you?" she asks, her voice full of disbelief. I reach my hand out to her and pass off the wadded sheet of paper. I sit down in the glider, kissing on Connor while she reads it. D.D. sits down on the oversized chair that Michael purchased for the room because he said he liked to sit and watch me feed the baby. Her face goes white. "I know what you're thinking, Hayden, and you can't."

"I don't have a choice."

"You do! You tell Devil and Skull and you let them—"

"Get Michael killed. If there's the smallest chance to save him, D.D.—*I have to take it.*"

"Will you listen to yourself? You're not some freaking Bruce Willis action figure. You're Hayden Graham. You have a small child depending on you. You don't have martial arts training and you suck at shooting a gun! You have a history of panic attacks!"

"I haven't had one in forever."

"You're going to therapy because of them!"

"But I'm better! I have to do this D.D. I can do it with you or without you, but I *am* doing it."

"Hayden this is crazy," she tries arguing with me one more time.

"Michael is my world, D.D. I have to do this. I have to give him every chance of survival."

"Are you listening to yourself? Don't you think Skull and Devil would have a better chance of getting Michael back?"

"Maybe if they managed to get inside the warehouse, but they won't get that chance unless I go first to distract them."

D.D. sighs looking at me. Maybe she finally understands that she's not going to change my mind. "What's your plan?"

"I need you to help me get out of here and then give me at least a thirty-minute head start before you tell Devil where I'm at."

"Gee is that all?"

"Well that and you know those things your brother gave you for self-defense when you moved out here? I need to borrow them."

"Because a Taser gun and brass knuckles will protect you from lunatics," she huffs.

"Well, I figure I can get that and my letter opener by whoever is watching."

"*A letter opener?*"

"Will you just please let me borrow them?"

"This is the stupidest, most asinine thing I have ever been involved in. You're basically asking me to help get my best friend killed. *Do you even realize that?* Jesus!" She's complaining the entire time, but she gathers the things I asked for out of her purse. "What the hell is going to happen to Connor if you die Hayden? Have you thought of that?"

"You'll take care of him and make sure he has a world that's filled with love," I tell her, trying to keep the pain and terror out of my voice.

"Hayden—" she says, her voice cracking as traces of tears begin to gather in her eyes.

"Please, D.D., I'm barely hanging on here. If you help me distract Diesel, let me take your car and you do your part, hopefully I'll be here for Connor *and* Michael."

"I give you thirty minutes and then send the cavalry. I got it. But do you honestly think these men are going to let you drive out of here on your own?"

"They will if they think I'm you..."

"Jesus. Okay tell me what you want me to do," she says. I'm still petrified, but I'm ignoring it and concentrating on the fact that finally I will be doing something to help Michael. He just has to hold on...

# ❧ 48 ❧

## HAYDEN

I've driven for an hour and a half, breaking all speed limits to try and keep my lead over Devil, Skull and the others. D.D. texted me almost an hour ago to tell me shit had hit the fan. I know they're following me now and that's good and bad. I need to get inside and keep Blade distracted while they move in. They know my plan by now, D.D. would have told them. I don't imagine that went over well—*or at all*.

I pull into the empty parking lot feeling nauseous. I sit there and let the feeling slowly ease before I move. Fear and adrenaline are warring with each other, but I'm managing to keep all signs of panic at bay. I guess therapy is helping after all.

I pull my hood down and shake my hair free. I needed all of Skull's men and Victor's to believe I was D.D., so I wore her hoodie—pushing all my hair inside of it. I was able to get away without anyone questioning it—even the man who had been standing close to her car. That was a close one, luckily it was one of the men from Skull's crew that I hadn't really talked to. When I pretended to talk on my cell, saying I was just leaving "Hayden's" and would be by to get my baby soon, the man stood back.

I have my letter opener hidden on the inside of my pants, with the handle wedged under my belt. I sharpened it with an electric knife sharpener I had in the kitchen. I wish it was sharper, but it will have to do. I left the brass knuckles. I didn't want to push my luck. The other items I have on my keychain. The Taser looks like a tube of lipstick and is miniature in size. D.D. swears it works as well as a regular one and I'm praying she's right. My pepper spray is on the chain too and at first glance it looks like a small flashlight with a fancy clip. I'm praying I get these by Blade—I'm scared I won't. I close my eyes and say a silent prayer. As I get out of the car I notice the scent of strawberries. It seems to get stronger and more vibrant the closer I get to the warehouse entrance. It seems completely out of place, I have no idea where it could be coming from, but I like it. It almost feels...*comforting*.

I get all the way to the front door—*alone*. I'm starting to think this is all a hoax. *Surely someone should have met me by now?* When I push on the door, it's not even locked. My nose curls at the scent that assaults me. It's so dark I can't see anything inside. Thankfully that warm, fresh scent of strawberries hits me again, slowly drowning out the other putrid smell.

It's completely dark inside. I feel along the inside door for a light switch—but find nothing. I need something to keep the door wedged open—I've lost hope Michael is inside, but maybe I can find something in there that will help locate him. I can't find anything big enough and between my nerves and the letdown of not seeing Michael...I'm feeling defeated. I want to scream, instead I can feel the tears want to fall. I refuse to let them. Michael wouldn't give up on me and I can't let this stop me either.

Maybe I have something in the car that will hold the door open. I take just a few steps, when a hand clamps down on my shoulder. I let out a squeal of shock, which turns into a cry of pain as the hand gets more forceful and turns me around. I expect to see Blade when he pulls me to face him. I'm surprised when it's not. I know this guy though—*Blade's brother*. Just as I come to terms with that realization, it hits me that this is the same man who came into the bakery and scared me.

*Why couldn't I have placed him then? It's my fault Michael is in this mess.*

He came by the club a couple of times, though I was never sure why. He and Blade clearly hated each other. If he's helping Blade against us, blood apparently trumps hate. Blade never allowed me to talk to the man. He even locked me in my room whenever his brother showed up. He told me he didn't want Drummer to hurt me. I didn't care as long as I had nothing to do with Blade or any of the club. Now, however, with Drummer looking down at me with those cold, dark eyes trained directly on me—I have to wonder if Blade wasn't right to separate us. Blade is evil, but vileness seems to seep from the pores of this man.

"I've been waiting for you, Hayden," he says with a dark smile, sending chills up my back, and causing the hair on the back of my neck to rise. I swallow down bile and the urge to vomit. I can't panic now. I have a plan. Devil and Skull will be here very soon. I just need to stall...and find Michael.

*Please be alive, Michael. Please.*

## ✤ 49 ✤

# BEAST

"Beast...Oh, Beast. Wake up! It's time for the fun to start," I hear Drummer's voice from a distance. I can't open my eyes. I try, but it seems impossible. Then I see a bright flash of light and realize they're already open, I just can't focus. I've given up hope of surviving, but if I ever manage to get my hands on that motherfucker I'll drag him into Hell with me.

*Help is coming. You need to be ready.*

That voice inside again. Is it Annabelle? It *sounds* like my daughter, but then again, I know I'm dying. I'm almost completely out of it most of the time. Starving, the torture, and being locked in a room with a rotting corpse, can't be a good combination. Add in that I still have a knife sticking out of my stomach, there's no vent or window, and I'm running a fever...chances are I'm completely delusional.

*Wake up!* The voice practically shouts in my head. I jerk from the force of it, but I'm not sure I care anymore. I just want to sleep.

*Hayden is here.*

"No," I mumble. It's a trick—*it has to be.*

"Michael?" Hayden's voice breaks out of the darkness and

seems to wrap around me. "Oh God! Michael!" I hear her anguished cry.

She's here. She's in this hell hole. *Drummer has her.* Fear slices through me like a razor-sharp blade. How did she get here? *Motherfucker!* Devil was supposed to take care of her. She was supposed to be safe. There's no way I can save her. I can't even fucking see her.

"No!" I scream. My voice sounds as bleak and hopeless as I feel.

"Get him down from there!" Hayden screams. I'm trying to shake myself out of the haze I'm in. I'm surprised I'm conscious. Then again, maybe I'm not. Maybe this is all just one fucked-up dream brought on by the fever. That would make more sense, because there's no way Hayden could be here. Devil wouldn't let me down that much...he knows to defend Hayden and Connor with his own life. *Motherfucker!* Is Connor here, too? It doesn't matter. It's just a dream—*a nightmare.*

*It's not real.*

"I like him hanging. He's like my trophy. A man should have a trophy when he catches his prey."

"Let him down!" Hayden screams again. I bet she's beautiful, even if she's just a figment of my imagination.

"You're not real," I mourn. I don't want her here, but I would have loved to have one more kiss, feel her arms around me one last time. Did she know how much she meant to me? I'm so fucked up in my head some days, I can't be sure.

"I'm real, Michael. Hold on please, honey? Just hold on, for me."

*I always did like it when she called me honey.* I never got those soft nicknames before from anyone other than Hayden. I never wanted them before her really. Her touch feels so cool against my skin. *And real.* She feels real, I hope I never wake up.

"I'm sure I told you to bring my nephew? Where is he? Did you purposely disobey me, Hayden? I may have to punish you."

Connor. *No!* I want out of this dream. I know how these things work and I can't stand Hayden getting hurt—even in a dream.

*I have to wake up...I have to.*

## 50

# HAYDEN

*Oh God.*

I thought I was prepared. I really did. I don't think anything could prepare me for the shape that Michael is in right now. I can't see that well, but Michael is hanging on a hook with rope and his poor wrists...

As if he can hear my thoughts, Drummer hits a switch and a light comes on behind Michael. It doesn't cast a lot of light toward us, but it highlights Michael perfectly. His head is down and he looks dead hanging there. His hair and beard are longer than before and his clothes are sticking to him, drenched from water. The part that chills me the most, is the blood that runs down Michael's arms and chest—all coming from his hands. There can't be any skin left on his wrists. *More scars.* Hasn't this beautiful man been put through enough? How is this fair? How can God, or fate or whatever let this happen to Michael over and over? He's suffered enough.

"I couldn't get Connor here without the men noticing. You had to know that. It was all I could do to slip away, but I'm here! Your brother can get his revenge on me. You need to let Michael go. He has nothing to do with Blade and the vendetta he has against me!" I yell, trying to lift on Michael to relieve some of the pressure off his poor wrists. It's useless, Michael is limp and he's not a small man. It's then I notice the knife in is stomach.

"This has nothing to do with Blade. Do you really think I'd go to such lengths to help someone I can't stomach? He was too weak to live."

I ignore Drummer. Michael has a small knife buried all the way to the hilt in his stomach. It's small, so it might not be very deep, but how long as it been there? *How has it not fallen out?* My first instinct is to remove it, but what if I do that and he bleeds out? I've heard of that happening...well...on television it's happened, but that could have truth in it.... I'm so scared and I don't know what else to do, but scream.

"You stabbed him? Let him down now!" I scream again. Drummer laughs. *He laughs.* I was afraid I would panic in this situation. I wasn't sure I could keep the panic attacks from coming back when I was under pressure. Yet, seeing Drummer laugh as Michael rambles in the background about dreams and being in Hell, all I can do is feed off my anger. I want to kill him. He hasn't checked my pockets or anything. He's an idiot and I find myself wishing I had brought the brass knuckles after all, because I'm pretty sure I could beat him to death at this point. Instead I turn slightly, fishing my keys out of my pocket. I grab the Taser and pray I remember exactly how it works. D.D. cautioned me to make sure I don't hit him where his clothes are thick and might stop how well the gun works.

"It's not your job to tell me to let him down. You have no power here, Hayden. You're going to be my new toy. I'm almost sad that Beast isn't more alert. I'd like him to see the pain you're in before I kill both of you," he taunts.

He's closer now too. It sounds like he's almost directly behind me. I turn on him and my eyes go wide when I see he's really just a couple steps away. I thought I'd have a little more room. I pull the trigger on the small device and see as sparks flair out and the leads connect to him. His body shakes and I'm feeling proud. Until he keeps advancing on me.

*Shit.*

## ❧ 51 ❧

## BEAST

*elp her! She needs your help! Daddy! Help her!*

I want to ignore the voice. I'm losing my mind. I know I am. Something in the desperation of it however, jars me. I shake my head, needing to clear it—wanting to try and help. I feel my whole body warm, encircled by that scent that has been comforting me in this hell. I can barely make out two figures in front of me. They're blurry, but I'd know Hayden's hair anywhere. *God.* I know she is a figment of my imagination, but I want to touch her. *I need to...touch...her...just...one...more...time.*

"Do you think I'm a pussy?" I hear Drummer laugh. He steps closer to Hayden—*too close.* "She would really get a kick out of the juice I'm shooting through you. Wouldn't she, Beast? Perhaps that is just one way I'll torture her while you're still breathing," he adds. I hear Hayden's gasp as he wrenches something from her hand. I'm not sure what they're talking about, but the idea of him doing anything to Hayden scares the fuck out of me. My anger helps me to center myself. I have to be alert. *I have to figure out what is going on.*

I find if I concentrate hard enough that things come into focus for short bursts. He's holding something, I can't see what it is.

207

Hayden is backing into me, her head hitting my knees. Her body is shaking, so whatever it is, I figure it's some kind of weapon. She moves to my side, still backing away from Drummer. He's saying something to her, that I can't make out what over the pain drumming in my head. It feels like I'm underwater and useless, but I have to do something. I force my body to move. It's not easy, everything feels like dead weight. The sting of pain through my wrists though runs down my arms and the agony it brings is enough to spur me so that I'm more alert. I hold onto that. I let the pain help me to focus, kicking out harder. I still can't hear what Drummer and Hayden are saying, but I now have enough momentum up that I kick my legs out on my next swing and capture Drummer's head between my legs. I scissor them, and tighten them to the point his head is trapped against my upper thigh, just above the knee. I try to focus my strength on my legs, but I know it won't last long. I can already feel my body weakening.

"Run Hayden! Run!" I growl—praying she does as I ask. I know instinctively this will be my last chance to give her freedom. I need Hayden to be free—even if she isn't real. I need that memory to take with me when I die. Hayden free and laughing. Hayden experiencing life and being happy. Hayden and Connor living on....

## 52

# HAYDEN

*ichael is alive!*
The joy that runs through me at that thought is something I can't describe. I knew he was still alive, sure. But, this shows he's more alert than I thought. He's fighting to survive. Drummer yells, doing his best to break free. I know he's going to soon. I can tell by the way that Michael is shaking. I don't have much time. I reach down and grab the letter opener that's wedged against my belt and pull it out. I'm so nervous the slick, silver handle nearly slides out of my hand. I tighten my hold, screaming. I only have his lower body because Michael's legs cover most of Drummer's head, neck and upper chest. I duck down quickly and I stab him once in the stomach, then twice, then three times. Drummer is screaming at me, and I feel his hands in my hair, ripping at it to get away from him. *My shot at saving Michael is gone.*

I can't accept defeat that easily. Michael wouldn't. Look at him now, still trying to help—even in the shape he's in. I can't give up.

Drummer slings me away, luckily I take the opener with me. I fall hard against the concrete, but my hand hits the forgotten keychain and Taser. I don't know how to reuse it. I'm not sure it's possible because wires are hanging from it now. I still have the mace, though, and at least it's military grade. I quickly hold it up and as Drummer advances toward me I spray it into his eyes.

"You fucking cunt!" he screams, bringing his arms up to guard his eyes. He takes several steps backwards. I'm trying to figure out what to do when Michael surprises me again. He takes one more swing and uses both legs to kick Drummer, propelling him backwards. He lands four or five feet away with a thud. "I'm going to fucking gut both of you!" he growls. For a minute I just stand there, amazed that Michael managed to help that much. My man is amazing. I look around and see an old crate. I drag it over and push it under Michael. His legs don't really stand firm under him, but I hope it takes a little of his weight away from his wrists.

I hear Drummer screaming. I look to see him standing up, breathing heavily, and stalking his way toward us. I frantically search around, trying to find anything to protect us with—besides this damn letter opener. *Why couldn't I have brought a pistol or something? It's not like Drummer even checked me for weapons! They hide those things in their shoes in the movies! I could have done that!* All thought stops when I see a body...a bloated body in the corner. I can't see much, but you can tell it's been here for a little while. How is it not stinking? I guess I can smell a little, but not like I should. *Just strawberries.*

I shake it off.

"You better run, while you still can. Michael's friends will be here any minute and when they find you—"

"You two will already be dead," he says, his eyes red and crying from the mace. The light casts an eerie glow on him and he looks even more menacing. I clench the letter opener tighter, trying to figure out exactly what to do.

"Why! Why would you do this? You don't even like Blade. What can he give you that would make you do this?"

"He can't give me nothing anymore," Drummer sneers. "He's rotting."

*I guess that answers the question of who the body is. Couldn't have happened to a nicer guy.*

"Then what's the point. Leave before the others get here. Leave Michael and me alone," I plead with him, but I know it's useless. He's deranged and completely unstable. *Where the hell are Devil and Skull?*

"Your *Michael* is the reason I didn't get to know my daughter. He's the reason she's dead. I'm going to take everything he cares about away from him and then kill him. It's my right!" He screams, the last sentence, lunging at me. Michael moves his body so it shoves me away, I stumble and fall to the ground, just in time to see Drummer collide with him. Before I can think about it I push my body up from the floor and I attack the back of Drummer— thrusting my homemade weapon into the back of his neck. I bury it as far as I can get it to go. It sinks remarkably easy and I hope that doesn't mean I've missed anything vital. I need time to figure out another attack. I stumble back a few steps, almost falling. I jumped slightly to reach Drummer's neck and I'm shaking so hard, it's hard to stand. I leave my weapon buried in his neck and pray.

At first, I think it's done nothing. Drummer brings his hands back to try and grab it. He doesn't say anything though—which is strange. Then he staggers backwards. I jump to the side, expecting him to turn around and attack. He doesn't. He keeps backing up and then all at once his body tips and he falls, crashing onto the concrete floor. When he lands, I take a cautious step towards him. *I think I killed him!*

"I think I killed him, Michael! I think he's dead!" I yell, kind of proud of myself. Then I scream as Skull and Devil pick that moment to break through the front door. "Help me get Michael down!" I yell. They look around stunned but come running toward us.

*Now I just have to pray Michael survives....*

## 53

## BEAST

I stare out the window, the view is the same as it's been every day for the last two weeks. A brick wall, which happens to be another wing in the hospital. I hate this place. I can't wait to get out. The nurse that came in this morning said I should get out tomorrow. Which is good. *I guess.* I've had so many antibiotics pumped through my system, I'm probably floating in them. I look down at a sleeping Hayden. She's everything I've always wanted in the world, and everything I thought I could never have. *Everything I shouldn't touch.* Even thinking the words, I reach down and let her hair curl around my finger. I still can't believe she set out to save me all on her own. I don't know how to deal with that. I'm used to women who try to save themselves and have no loyalty. I think Hayden has too much. How she could even share a trace of blood with Pistol is beyond me. When I think of all of the men who have abused her trust, hurt her, and tried to destroy her—her courage blows my mind.

*How could they not see how precious and rare she is? She should be cherished and pampered her entire life.* It's something I looked forward to doing...*before.*

"How long have I been out?" Hayden asks with a sleepy smile, sitting up to look at me.

"You need to go home and rest. Connor needs you," I tell her again for the hundredth time. She's running herself ragged going back and forth between the hospital and home. I ordered Skull and Devil and even Victor to keep her home. They didn't listen. Devil went back with his men. Diesel called and checked on me. He had to leave before I got out. He's got a mess on his hands dealing with his son. Someone keeps trying to kidnap him. It's gotten to the point that Diesel has taken him out of preschool and is now interviewing nannies and teachers, so he can keep his son at his club, under constant protection. I can't say as I blame him. I'd probably do the same.

"Will you quit trying to get rid of me, Michael?" Hayden responds. Sadness comes on her face and I hate it. I hate that I'm causing her more pain. *I just don't know how to make her understand.*

"Hayden. Connor needs you. You have a new son and a business. The last thing you need to do is be here, trying to take care of me," I respond, refusing to look at her.

"Why are you pushing me away, Michael?" she asks, hurt thick in her voice.

"I'm not," I lie.

"You are. You have been ever since your fever broke and the infection began to leave your body. You've been cool to me at best, and you keep trying to get me to leave. My place is here with you. If the roles were reversed, you would be here for me. So, just stop it already."

"Hayden, I just think now that you're out of danger and things are back to normal, it'd be better if I go back to North Carolina."

"Then I'll get Connor ready and we'll leave with you," she says and guilt weighs heavily on me. I could do something stupid so that she leaves, but I don't have that in me. I pushed her away once and it almost killed me to see the pain she was in. I can't do that again. "Will you look at me!" she demands and I do, deciding it's time I just give her honesty.

"Hayden, I'm not good enough for you or Connor."

"You're full of shit. You fought to save me. You fought to survive. Why are you trying to ruin it all now? Why are you pushing me away, after working so hard to get me to let you back in? Talk to me Michael, because I know there's something. Either that, or you were lying to me when you told me you loved me and Connor."

"I love you both."

"Then what the hell is wrong?" she questions, frustrated.

"I think I'm broken, Hayden. I don't think it's safe for me to be around you or Connor."

"Are you insane?" she almost screeches.

"I think I might be," I confess and slowly I see her face fill with confusion. She reaches out and grabs my hand. I had forgotten how great that felt. A moment later her thumb is tracing the deep jagged scar and I have to close my eyes at the emotion that causes.

*I love her. God help me, I love her.*

## ❧ 54 ❧

## HAYDEN

Of all the things I thought I'd have to face, this wasn't it. I knew something was going on with Michael—but I had no idea what. I didn't expect him to try and push me away though. I'm tired, I'm cranky and the last thing I want to do is fight with Michael.

"Michael, Connor didn't sleep well last night and I'm tired—"

"That's just another reason you need to go home," he interrupts me. At this point, I'm just done.

"Quit being a stupid ass. I'm not leaving you. I don't know why at this point, because clearly you're completely stupid, but I happen to love you. I fought to keep you with me and no one—*not even* you, will get me to change my mind at this point. You told me you loved me. You wanted to be Connor's father, so it's time for you to man up and stop trying to get out of your promises."

"I'm not trying to get out of anything, damn it."

"Well, it sure looks like it from where I'm sitting," I respond, liking that I see a spark of anger from him. That's much better than his eyes avoiding mine.

"I'm trying to be honest with you!"

"Then, I'm sorry honey, but it's not translating. I need you to speak English."

"There's something wrong with me," he grumbles, and I find my first smile.

"Michael, I knew that when I fell in love with you, despite your sour disposition and your tendency to grunt instead of speak."

"I'm being serious, Hayden. I think there's something wrong with me." I see a flash of fear cross his face. I tighten my hold on his hand, while pushing his hair out of his face with my other one. "You're always trying to hide this beautiful face from me," I chastise him gently.

"Hayden—"

"Talk to me, Michael. *Really* talk to me. What's going on in that head of yours?" I ask him, praying I'm finally getting through to him.

"I've been talking to Annabelle," he confesses, his dark eyes troubled.

"Your daughter?"

"Yeah. She is my daughter, Hayden. It doesn't matter if I didn't father her."

"I'm sorry Drummer told you...that you had to find out like that, I mean."

"I kind of already knew—mostly. But it didn't matter, Hayden. I already loved Annabelle—she was mine in every way that counted," he stresses. It's almost as if he's pleading his case to me, which is the last thing I want.

"I know that, Michael! I'm the last person you ever have to explain that to! You will always be Connor's father, and I have no doubt in my mind you doted on Annabelle. Is that what's going on? Are you worried about being Connor's dad? Because I can understand if you don't want to take—"

"No absolutely not. I love Connor. I love you, Hayden. I never want you to question that," he interrupts, and I do feel better, but also more confused.

"Then what is this about?"

"When Drummer had me tied up...I heard Annabelle. She would talk to me, Hayden. She told me you were coming. Hell, she told me when you were there."

I take a deep breath.

"Honey, you were—"

"Don't try to tell me I was delirious, or that things like that happen under stress. I know that, but this was different. This was more. I felt her, Hayden...I heard her in my head...and I could..."

"Could what?"

"Smell her. The scent of her shampoo...it blanketed me in that hellhole. The place smelled like strawberries constantly and it's not the first time it has happened. That day your store was being robbed, it happened then, too, and then again when you went into labor. I know it sounds crazy, I do...*but it happened just the same.*"

"Michael," I start and then stop. "You're not going crazy."

"Hayden, you don't understand. I don't want to be around you and Connor if something happens and I snap. What if I hurt one of you? I wouldn't do it intentionally, but what if I didn't realize what was really happening? What if—"

"Michael that day I came to the warehouse, I smelled the strawberry scent, too. I never really smelled how bad it was inside that room. I couldn't understand why Devil and all of the other men were talking about it so much. I promise you, Michael. I completely believe you."

"Do you think Annabelle—"

"Honey, I don't know. Who am I to say she did or didn't?" I quickly interrupt him. I need to make him understand something. "I will tell you what I do know, beyond a shadow of a doubt."

"What's that?"

"When you love someone so deeply that it feels like it lives inside of you? That kind of love never dies. It lives on forever. Annabelle will live on because of your love, and I think if there was any way she could reach out to her Dad when he needed her? She would. Because a love like that is special. Unconditional love is something death can never claim."

"I let her down, Hayden," he confesses, his voice full of shame and hurt. The tears sliding down his face. He's not sobbing. They're just slow running tears that keep dropping. His dark eyes look so bleak my heart breaks. Michael has so much pain inside of him, how can I ever help him so that he can heal?

"You did not, Michael, we—"

"I wasn't able to save her. I was her father! I was supposed to protect her, keep her safe, and I failed. I failed, and she died," he says so quietly, I have to strain to hear him.

"You did not let her down. Jan had no business taking her out of the club when you guys were on lockdown. She knew not to. Michael—"

"I knew what kind of woman Jan was, and I still wanted her around to help raise Annabelle. I kept her around so I could live my life without having to change or give up one damn thing. I—"

"You're talking stupid," I all but growl. I tighten my hand on his so tight his skin turns white from my grip. "You're only human, just like the rest of us. You did the best you could do. You loved Annabelle. You loved her completely. Skull told me there were nights when she was sick that you would sit up all night with her, just so she would get her medicine on time. He said there were times when you would get in, after being gone before daylight, and the rest of the men would crash because they were so tired, but you would go to Annabelle and spend the entire evening with her playing blocks and holding her until she fell asleep."

"But..."

"He said you'd go days without sleep, just so you were always there for Annabelle. He said you wouldn't allow yourself to fail the club or your daughter. You were one of the few men he could always depend on."

"I should have disappointed the club!" he yells, and I wish he could stop raking himself over the coals. "I should have taken my daughter away and never let anything touch her. I should have kept her away from—"

"Michael, stop. None of us knows what God's plan is. If you

had left the club maybe she would have lived, maybe she would have died a different way, honey. We don't know."

"Don't say it, Hayden. Don't say it was her time. Don't. I hate that shit. People say that crap all the time. *It was just her time. God, had a different plan for her.* The first thing people do when you lose someone you love, is spout that crap. My favorite is, *He probably took her now because if he hadn't she may have died from cancer or something worse later on.* It's all bullshit. All of it! I'm not sure there is a God, but if there is, who in the hell is he to decide if I can or can't have my daughter? Who in the hell is he to take my daughter away from me. I loved her, Hayden. I loved her," he cries and that's when the sobs start. They shake his body and finally, years of grief begins to trickle out.

I get on the bed and curl into him, holding him with all the strength I have—letting him cry. His head lays on my chest and he holds onto me while he cries. Tears are falling down my face too. Tears for Annabelle...but, mainly my tears are for Michael...for the pain and hurt that is embedded so deeply inside of him. I know now that all of it will never leave him. There's no way it could.

"I know you loved her, Michael. I know you loved her," I whisper to him gently, letting my tears fall unchecked and praying my body absorbs every trace of his.

"Why Annabelle? Why, Hayden? Why couldn't it be me? Why can't my daughter be here discovering how beautiful life is? Why can't she be wrapped in love and feel the sun..."

"How do you know she's not, Michael?" I ask, pulling away enough so I can look in his eyes. I kiss his forehead, because I can't resist that simple touch. "How do you know, Michael?"

"Because she's not here—"

"You said that you felt her with you. That every time you needed her, you smelled her shampoo, and you could feel her. Just because you can't see her, that doesn't mean she wasn't real."

"But—"

"There's no other way to explain it. I could smell the strawberries too, remember? I felt the warmth when there was no possible explanation for it. Who is to say she wasn't right there with you, helping her Daddy in any way she could? You know it was her in your heart. You've already decided that. Keep that inside of you, Michael. Because that's proof that somewhere she lives on."

"I want her here..."

"None of us want to lose someone we love, Michael. But, if this is possible, who is to say Annabelle isn't happy? That what she sees is even more beautiful? That she's not completely happy touching the stars?"

"Do you really think that's possible?"

"I think where there is love, anything is possible, Michael. You taught me that."

I'd like to say my words reached him, but in that moment our small sterile hospital room goes from smelling like antiseptic to strawberries. I see Michael's eyes widen in disbelief, and my tears begin falling harder than his.

"I smell them, too," I whisper, knowing he'll understand. "*I smell them too.*"

He pulls up looking around the room and though he doesn't see anything, I don't think it matters. He pulls me even closer and buries his head in the side of my neck, his hold on me is a tight bruising force—*and it's never felt so good.*

"I love you, Hayden. With everything I am, I love you," he whispers, and it feels like a vow.

"I love you, Michael. I always will," I respond and that *is* a vow. One I will gladly honor the rest of my life and whatever comes after.

## 𝕷 55 𝕰

# BEAST

### TWO WEEKS LATER

"A re you sure I can't talk you into coming home, mi hermano," Skull asks again—for probably the tenth time in the last hour. We clasp hands and I pound him on the back.

"I don't belong there anymore man. I have a home here now," I tell him, feeling those words through every inch of my being. I look back over my shoulder and see Hayden and Connor sitting on the porch. Hayden is laughing at Connor, and he's reaching out with his chubby little hands to try and capture her hair. "I have a family here," I finish, turning back around. There's sadness in his eyes, but then I understand, because I'm a little sad about closing this chapter of my life too. We've shared a lot of life's ups and downs together, but the simple truth is, I'm not the same person anymore. Losing Annabelle broke me, and the pieces are slowly coming back together, but they're completely different now. I'm not Beast...I'm Michael...*Hayden's Michael.*

"Si. You have a family. I'll miss you my friend. You always have a home with us," he says and I know he means that shit. He dropped everything to travel half way across the U.S. for me. I won't forget that. If I think about it too long, the truth of it chokes me up.

"I'll miss you too, Skull. I'll always be around. Nothing separates a brother," I answer, my voice gruff.

"Not even the fires of Hell," we finish together.

"Take care, asshole," he says, with a wink and gets on his bike. I say goodbye to the others and stand there watching each of them drive off.

"Are you going to miss them?" Hayden asks, and I'm surprised to find her standing beside me with Connor on her side.

"Yeah, but my life is here now," I tell her truthfully, wrapping my hand around her shoulder and bringing her closer.

"I don't want you to regret—"

"I regret nothing. I have everything a man could ask for right here," I assure her, and I'm telling the truth. I would give anything to have Annabelle here with us. I doubt that will ever change. My daughter is a part of me, she always will be, but I have to keep living. I owe it to Annabelle...*I owe it to myself.*

"How about a dirty diaper? Are you asking for one of those? Cause, that's exactly what we have," she laughs. "I'll take him to the nursery and clean him up. It's almost bottle time."

"I'll take him," I tell her, already reaching for Connor.

"You don't have to do that honey. I can—"

"You can get ready and meet me in our bedroom. Connor and I have this, and I'll get him to sleep. Then I'm coming after you, woman." I wink.

"Michael," she whispers, her gray eyes large and expressive, her face flushing with heat. Last night I did what I could to prepare her for tonight. I'm claiming her. It's time I started living and showing Hayden that she's the center of my world. *Everything leads back to her.*

I bend down and give her a quick kiss. "Don't keep me waiting," I tell her with a smile. Then, I turn with Connor in my arms and walk back inside the house.

## ❧ 56 ❧

# BEAST

"I don't think I'll ever get tired of this view," I tell Hayden as I walk into our bedroom. She's lying on the bed in her robe. Her hair is brushed until it shines, but that's not what makes me catch my breath. It's the smile on her face and the way those gray eyes shine that do that. I never get tired of the way Hayden smiles, or how she lets her happiness radiate for everyone to see. *For me to see.*

"Connor sleeping?"

"Like a baby. Though I don't get that phrase, because I had forgotten just how much babies do *not* sleep," I joke, leaning against the door and crossing my arms.

"You aren't kidding. The bags under my eyes grow daily," she laughs.

"You look beautiful," I tell her and it's the truth. There's not a day that goes by that I don't look at her and think that I'm the luckiest son of a bitch to ever walk the face of the earth. "You know I love our boy, Hayden?" I question her and her face instantly takes on that dreamy look whenever I claim her or Connor. She still doesn't get that I'm the one who should get down on my knees and thank my lucky stars that I have them.

"I do," she whispers.

"Good. But I don't want to talk about him right now. He's the last thing I want to talk about."

"Oh, but..." her face clouds in confusion.

"I want you to stand up and take that robe off."

Her mouth drops open, forming an '*o*'. She stands up without questioning me, in fact her smile deepens. My eyes are drawn to her hands as she slowly undoes the belt on her robe. The hot pink silk begins to part showing me just mere traces of her breasts and a glimpse of her sweet pussy. I grunt, not hiding my displeasure that she hasn't removed it yet. I undo my pants, sliding the zipper down to give my cock room. It seems like I haven't been inside of Hayden in years. She watches the zipper separate, her tongue coming out to lick her lips. I want to groan at the promise in her eyes.

She slowly takes the robe off, letting it pool at her feet. I yank my shirt off in response. She takes a step toward me, at the same time I close the distance between us. Her eyes lock with mine as her hands go to the waist of my jeans. She pushes them down over my hips and then goes to her knees, pulling them further down. She looks up at me, my cock thrusts out towards her, as her hand encircles my shaft, and she gives it one, slow stroke. I grunt as she stops. She holds the head of my cock tightly and lets her finger slide against the pre-cum gathered on the tip. Her eyes never leave mine, as she drags her tongue through it.

"Suck me," I order, unable to resist. She holds my cock still and then slowly, inch by inch my cock disappears between those thick lips of hers. *Motherfucker! It feels like heaven.* My hand tangles in her hair, as she begins to back off my shaft, unable to take it all in her mouth. "Get it nice and wet, Beauty. You better fucking have it drenched, because I'm taking your fucking ass next. I'm not stopping until I'm buried inside of you and filling you full of my cum." I use my rough hold in her hair to push her back on my cock. Hayden hums her approval and I feel it vibrating through my fucking balls. She's trying to choke on my damned cock. Every stroke, she takes me further and further into her throat. *Christ!* I could come just like this, fucking her face, taking my pleasure, filling her mouth so full of cum that it runs down her neck and body. Just imagining it makes my hunger for it indescribable. Yet, that's not what I want right now. Afterwards, maybe, *but not right now.*

"Michael," she whispers. The word is almost unrecognizable because before she even gets the breath out, she's devouring me. She wants more, it's in her tone and the way those stormy eyes are pleading

"Stand up," I demand, pulling her off of me. My voice is so dark and full of hunger that I don't recognize it. I can see her body shiver in reaction. She gets to her feet, using my body as support. Her fingers bite into my hips, and just that one touch makes me want to throw her down on the bed and fuck her until neither of us can move. "Turn around, Hayden," I bark. She slowly turns, her neck stretching so her eyes can stay on mine until the last minute, when she's completely facing the bed.

I let my hands begin at her neck, caressing it slowly, and trying to memorize every inch of her body. I move to her shoulders, letting my fingers press into the skin, teasing her before moving down her back.

"God, Michael, that feels so good," she moans. I lean in close, letting my breath warm her neck, and placing a kiss where it meets her shoulder. I slide my tongue against her hammering pulse point, tasting the salty skin I find there, and needing more. I bite into her ear and get rewarded with her soft gasp of surprise.

"Bend over the bed, Beauty. I want to see what you're about to give me," I whisper in her ear.

I can feel her body tremor, but she leans over the bed—letting her hands act as a brace. I pet her, dragging my hand through her hair and down her back, admiring the curve of it. I place small kisses along her spine, teasing her as well as myself. I want to make this last as long as I can. I continue downward with my kisses, my teeth raking across the cheek of her ass and then biting into the fleshy mound on one side. I spank the other side with my hand and watch as it blossoms a bright pink, instantly.

"Oh God!" she cries out, as my fingers push between her cheeks and find the end of the plug. I buried it deep inside of her ass this morning, after I woke her up with my tongue buried inside of her pussy. I begin to pull on the plug, slowing dragging it from her ass, then thrusting it back in. Her body lurches forward. Her legs shake and I watch, as her fingers dig into the mattress. Once she's taken the plug back in, I turn it, twisting it inside of her, until she calls out my name. "Michael!" she yells, and there is nothing better in the world than to hear her call out for me.

"This ass is nice and stretched for me now," I praise. "Are you ready for me, Beauty?" I ask, repeating my motions again.

"Please," she whimpers, her face buried in the mattress as she thrusts back into me. She's more than ready, which is good because I can't hold off any longer.

I carefully take out the plug. My eyes are glued to the way those tiny muscles clench around it, trying to hold it in. I groan imagining just how fucking good she's going to feel against my cock. I put the plug on the black velvet towel that I laid across the nightstand this morning. There's a small, red box there too—along with a white tube of lube. I placed it all there on purpose. I wanted Hayden to see it when she got out of bed. I wanted to tease her. I told her not to open the box. She may have, I don't know—either way it would have stayed on her mind all day, and that's all that matters.

I open it now to reveal a miniature vibrator that is shaped like a silver bullet. There's a small button on the edge and I click it, to turn it on. It begins quivering gently in my hand. I move it against the lips of her pussy. She jumps at first, whether from surprise or the slick feel of the vibrator, I'm not sure. I know it has to be cold against her heated flesh. I slide it between her lips. She's so wet her cum is already dripping on my fingers. She wants this—almost as much as I do. I let the tip of the bullet glide against her cli, as she thrusts her ass hard against me.

"You like that, sweetheart?" I ask her. I pet her back with one hand, while still using the other to tease her with the vibrator.

"Michael, I need to come," she whimpers, practically begging. I push the switch on the end with my thumb again, increasing the speed. Hayden lets out a long, pleading whimper, as I tease her clit over and over in small circles. She comes against my fingers. Her sweet juices bathe my fingers, as her body jerks and trembles. There's no fucking way I can keep holding back. I click the switch on the end two more times, which brings the device to a hard pulsation that slowly fades, before it repeats. Once I'm sure it's doing exactly what I want it to, I push it gently inside of her pussy. "Oh, fuck," she whimpers. "That feels so good. Michael! It feels so...I need more baby," she rambles. Her head is pushed down into the mattress, her hips moving back and forth.

"Ride it, Hayden. Ride the fucking hell out of it. I'll give you more in a minute, Beauty," I assure her, my voice more of a groan than anything else, as I watch her fuck herself.

*Jesus.*

I grab the lube off the nightstand and I savagely rip the cap off, squeezing the gel into my hand. I take my cock roughly in my hand, stroking it and making sure every inch is covered in the lube. I squeeze out a little more—just on two fingers. The entire time I'm watching as Hayden's body moves back and forth trying to ride the small vibrator, but never getting enough to push her over the edge.

I grab her hip and hold her forcibly, refusing to let her move. Then, I carefully begin to paint the opening of her ass with the lube. I pull one of her cheeks out, to better access the tight ringed opening.

"Michael," she whispers, too lost in passion to be afraid of what's coming—and that's exactly what I want.

"So, fucking perfect, Hayden. You're everything," I rumble from above her, just as my fingers slide into her ass, working the lube inside. The plug has loosened her up, more than doing its job. She's still so incredibly tight that I know I won't be able to last long. I pull my fingers apart, testing her body, while deep inside. When I'm satisfied she's ready, I slowly pull my fingers out. "Don't let me hurt you, Beauty," I whisper, because I'm not sure I have the self-control to pay attention. I want to bury myself deep inside of her and fuck her hard.

"You won't hurt me," she whispers, her faith in me unwavering, which is as much of a miracle as anything else. *She's my world.*

I slowly guide my cock to the entrance, pushing in a little at a time. Her muscles immediately clamp down and I find myself moving a hand back to her pussy, searching out the vibrator and finding the button to change the speed again. The next function brings a steady, pulsating that causes her ass to thrust back. The head of my cock pops through the muscles, and I cuss under my breath, as I force myself to stop. Now that I'm inside, even a little —I move both hands to her hips to steady her. I don't stop her from moving, however; she keeps thrusting back and each time she takes a little more of my dick. It's an exercise in torment to keep holding back, and I quickly reach my limit.

I push into her, closing my eyes, as she takes inch after inch of my cock deep into her ass. Her body stops moving when I get about half way in and her breathing has changed.

"Am I hurting you?" I rumble. I don't know how, but I'll find a way to hold myself back if I am.

"I just feel...so...full..." she breathes.

"Does it feel good?" I ask her, as my hand tangles into her hair. Needing to touch it.

"Yes. *Really* good," she whimpers, moving her body back and taking more of me.

I pull away, almost removing my dick and then slowly thrust forward again. I do this several times and each time she takes me a little further inside. I bend over her, fucking her harder, feeling mistakenly powerful. She's the one who holds all the power. This woman could destroy me. Soon we're fucking like two animals mating. I feel the moment she orgasms again, the movement of her muscles and the vibrating in her pussy, wrap around my cock almost as much as the tight muscles of her ass.

I yank her hair back with my hold, knowing it will hurt, but beyond the ability to be careful. I ram her body with mine. Her ass cushions me while I fuck her.

"Hayden!" I growl out, as my balls tighten. I yank my cock out when my cum starts jetting out. I finish outside of her. I jack off in my hand and watch while my cum streams against her asshole, then, further down her ass cheeks and up her back. I cover her in *my* cum, losing my breath at how fucking beautiful she looks coated in it. Once I finish, and the last drop is drained, I use my hand to rub it into her skin.

I push between her legs and yank the vibrator out. Hayden has collapsed against the bed, completely exhausted. Her body keeps jerking from the force of her last orgasm. I rub my cum against her pussy, needing it there too.

"So fucking beautiful," I mumble, my lips finding the back of her neck as I lay on my side half on her, half off.

"Love you...Michael," she whispers brokenly, still panting for breath.

"I love you too, Beauty. I'll take us to the shower as soon as I can feel my legs again."

"Okay," she says softly, but she goes lax in my arms.

There's a certain amount of pride involved when you fuck your woman so hard she falls asleep. I kiss the back of her neck again. Then regretfully, rise and go into the bathroom to run a tub of water, making sure to add some fragrant salts that will help with the soreness.

*Time to pamper my woman*...and I might be a bastard, but I'm already thinking of fucking her again too.

## 57

## HAYDEN

I come awake slowly. My hand automatically goes to the side of the bed where Michael sleeps. I frown when it's empty. I turn to look at the alarm clock and wince. It's after ten in the morning. I slept through Connor's cries. It's no wonder, after the workout that Michael gave me last night. Sex with him has always been amazing, but last night for the first time, I felt like I got all of Michael—heart and soul. He held nothing back. A smile plays lazily on my lips as I remember the night and as tired as I am, I feel my body trying to come back to life. Apparently when Michael is involved, I'm insatiable.

I sit on the side of the bed, deliciously sore all over. When I stand, I swear my stomach is actually sore. I go to the full-length mirror hanging on the wall, and I can see small bruises on different parts of my body. I remember how I got each of them and I can feel wetness begin to pool between my legs. Michael's destroyed me. The thought makes me grin. I grab my robe off the floor and put it on, cinching the tie at my waist. I run my hand through my hair, combing my fingers through it. I need to check on Connor, then find Michael and food... If I'm this hungry from our play time last night, that man has to be starved. He has the stamina of a triathlete—well if my body was an Olympic field. *That* thought makes me giggle.

I stop at the doorway to Connor's room. Michael is rocking Connor in the glider. There's something so precious about this big, huge, scarred, inked-covered, brute of a man holding this tiny child in his arms so delicately. Little Connor's eyes are round and wide and his fingers are only able to half-way wrap around one of Michael's. I commit the sight to memory, knowing I'll never get enough of it.

"You would have loved your sister. She had beautiful blue eyes just like you," Michael whispers. "Mommy says your eyes will probably change when you get a little older, though."

*The smile on my face stretches to the point it's almost painful.*

"When you get older I'll tell you all about her. She would have loved you. She always wanted a little brother or sister to play with. You can help me work on your Mommy and maybe she'll agree to move a little further out in the country. We'll have a fishing pond where we can catch fish and I'll build us a big deck, so we can all sit on it at night and watch the stars. Your sister would like knowing I have someone to watch the stars with again. I never knew love until Annabelle. She taught me how to love and that's a good thing. Do you know why?" Michael asks a completely captivated Connor. Connor coos back, which is about all he can do, but I think just like me, he really wants to know the answer. "Because of her, I can love your Mommy like I do. And I do love her. I'll spend the rest of my life loving her and making sure she has everything she wants," he says and I feel those sloppy, happy tears which Michael can always get me to produce, start to slide from my eyes. "And I love you, Connor. Daddy will always love you and give you everything you want. I promise," he finishes, kissing Connor's forehead.

Michael has no idea that he did just give me everything I could ever want. In this small room, I have everything.

"And you want a big farm with a pond, don't you, Daddy's boy?"

I don't know if Connor can understand, but he lets out the first squeal he's ever given, so I think he does.

*Looks like I'm moving out to the country with my boys.*

"Thank you, Annabelle," I whisper. "Thank you for trusting your Daddy with me and for teaching him to love. I promise, I'll never take it for granted," I whisper off into space. I don't know if she hears me, but I pray she does and it could be just my imagination, but the warmth that I feel surrounding me in that moment leads me to believe she does.

*And she approves.*

# EPILOGUE

## HAYDEN

*Three Months Later—On the new farm.*

I look at the piece of paper I hold in my hands. I'm nervous. I think I know how Michael will react, but our lives have barely begun calming down. Poor Michael seems to get one hit to the gut after another. I know finding out he wasn't Annabelle's true father hurt him. He might have been doubtful about it all along, thanks to Jan's cruelty. She actually told people that Annabelle was Michael's brother's child. *Which is just one of many reasons he and Michael never talk anymore.* Michael suspected it all, but he had never had it confirmed. Having it thrown in his face the way he did, having his past come back to the point we almost lost each other, it wounded him deeply. I'm so grateful that he's held on to me and to our family. He has never pulled away from me. He's never shut me out and he has loved me and Connor with all he has.

We moved to the small farm on the outskirts of town about two months ago. It has a private fishing pond and an old cabin, that Michael is slowly transforming. His first step was to add on two more bedrooms and a large great room for Connor to play in.

It's a beautiful room, covered in rustic wood and lots of windows that overlook the pond. The second thing he did was to add a huge deck onto it. True to his word, every night the three of us go out and watch the stars. It's an amazing life—a perfect life, and I know Michael is happy.

Still, there are times when I look over at him and I can see the shadows of his past, the sadness in his eyes that he tries to keep hidden. Those are the times I do my best to give him more and fill up his life with our family and all the love I have in my heart for him.

That day I decided to go to the warehouse alone, wasn't an easy decision. I knew Connor needed his mother. Yet, I also knew that I couldn't live, I couldn't be the person Connor truly deserved as a mother—without Michael. I would die for either...*any* of my family, if it meant keeping them safe and happy. But without Michael, I would wither away inside. There would be nothing left to give Connor. So, even though Michael still gets upset with me for my decision to go to him that day, I'd do it again. *In a heartbeat.*

The house is quiet as I walk through the kitchen, but I can hear Michael talking to our son, his voice so full of love, I ache. The words are nonsense, just cooing to Connor and calming him. Michael's gruff voice is soft and low. He loves Connor and he loves him in a way that Connor will never doubt that Michael is his Daddy. That's special. It takes a man—a *real* man—to have the capacity to love a child that isn't his by blood, but love him as if he were. I never dreamed in a million years that the day Michael Jameson stopped across from my house, to relieve himself on my small patch of wildflowers, would become the day my life would change forever. I would say it became the best day of my life—but that's not true. Every day spent with Michael and Connor is better than the last.

I look down at the paper in my hands, and I feel the tears well up in my eyes. *Better than the last.* I make it to Connor's nursery and watch my big bear of a man bend over Connor's crib, placing our child there to sleep. I'm reminded even more forcefully how blessed I am. Here in this room, *I have everything.*

If I looked back on my past and knew that I'd find myself where I am at now, with this beautiful baby and a man that I love irrevocably...*love in a way I didn't truly know existed*...I would go through it all again. It's not pretty, but then maybe some stories aren't meant to be pretty. That way when you get to the happily-ever-after part, you appreciate it more. You realize how truly sweet and rare it is. You realize it's something that you will never take for granted.

In real-life you don't always get fairytales. You don't always get the love and the happily-ever-afters. You get pain. You get tragedy. That's what our story is—Michael's and mine. Our story was messy, dirty, painful, and even tragic. *Until it wasn't.*

I move my hand to my stomach and close my eyes as I smile. I hear Connor laughing and my eyes go to my family. *My family.* The thing about our story is there is no grand finish. There is nothing that says, *"the end."*

"Da Da!" Connor squeals and those tears begin to fall from my eyes, but happy tears are more than allowed.

Yeah. There's no end in sight for Connor and me.

*Our story is just beginning.*

# EPILOGUE

## BEAST

"Da' Da'," Connor squeals from his crib. Pride and something very close to joy floods through me. Connor's first words. His very first words and...*they're mine.* I look down at him, and he's reaching up to me with that sweet smile of his. He keeps kicking his legs and if he was able he'd jump to me right now. "Da' Da'!" he cries again and I bend down and pick him up.

"Did he just call you daddy?" Hayden shrieks out, her voice full of happiness. I turn around to look at her and she's smiling so big it has to hurt.

"I think he did," I tell her, emotion so thick it clogs my voice.

"My smart little baby!" Hayden coos to Connor, kissing his cheeks and her palm presses against my hand, her fingers curl down. I look down at that and I know this will be a moment I remember for the rest of my life. Our hands linked, holding a six-month old Connor, our Connor. He's ours. Hayden gave me that and so much more. She gave me a family. A home.

Before Hayden came into my life I was barely alive. I was dying from the inside out. It was just a matter of time before I worked up the courage to end it all. That's what I came to North

Carolina to do, I can admit that now. But then something happened. *No.* Someone happened. *Hayden happened.* She stormed into my life in a rainstorm, riding a chainsaw and my life has never been the same since. Hayden somehow resuscitated me. Taught me how to breathe again. Until eventually, I was breathing and taking in each new day. She made me want to see the sun come up, instead of hating it. She made me want to survive another day, just to see what she gave me next. Because that is Hayden—*she gives with her whole heart.* First she gave me a reason, she gave me her body, she gave me love, and then slowly she gave me life. I once thought Hayden came into my life to teach me. That she was here so I could learn to breathe again. I know now that I was wrong. She is a gift that taught me to live. I learned to live again, all because of this beautiful, fiery woman, with eyes the color of a stormy sky.

Connor giggles in that cute baby laugh that never fails to make me laugh with him. Hayden tugs on my hand and I look down at her.

"It sure is a good thing you're such an awesome father," she tells me and even with my happiness, there's a tug of sorrow—that even Hayden, as well as she knows me, doesn't realize her words cause. I'm slowly coming to terms with my past. There's so much that I would go back and change if I could. The simple truth is...*I can't.* I see things clearer now, because I know the outcome. We aren't afforded that luxury in life. Annabelle's death was tragic, it was horrible, but I tried to save her. I loved her and it doesn't matter our circumstances. I was her father and I would have laid down my life for her. I think she knows that. I don't know if the voices I heard were real, but I like to think they were. I know I feel her with me so strongly at times, there's no other explanation. Hayden was right when she told me love is too powerful for death to claim. It lives on. Annabelle lives on.

"I love you, Hayden," I tell her, the emotion so overwhelming the words are just too simple to describe my emotion.

"That's good, because I have something to tell you," she says, smiling. She pulls on my hand and leads me to the living room. We sit down together and I balance Connor on my leg.

"What's going on?" She's not been feeling well for a few days and she went to the doctor this morning. I wanted to take her, but Connor is just getting over an ear infection and we didn't want to risk exposing him to germs from the doctor's office. Hayden and I haven't allowed anyone but us watch over Connor. He's too precious and we've seen too easily how things can happen. Whatever is happening now, the two of us can handle it together. I refuse to let fear get a foothold here.

"Well, I went to the doctor this morning and everything checked out fine," she says with a smile. I breathe a sigh of relief.

"Then why are you getting sick? You are going to have to shut down the bakery. Running a business and caring for Connor is just becoming too much."

"Now you're talking crazy, Michael. I'm not giving up my shop."

"Then at least let D.D. take over more responsibility," I grumble, figuring it's useless. Hayden is a control freak when it comes to her business, but it's time she starts putting herself first.

"Well on that we can agree," she says, shocking me.

"No argument?" I ask, thinking she's giving in way too easily.

"None. I don't think I have a choice. When our baby gets here, I'm going to be way too busy."

"Good. I'm glad you're listening to me—did you just say, *our baby?*"

"Mm hmm," she confirms, biting her lip and grinning.

"You're pregnant?" I whisper. Connor is only a little over six months old, but we haven't been taking precautions. I'll be the first to admit that's my fault. I don't like anything between us. We've discussed birth control, but both of us kind of just shrugged it off. If I'm honest, I like Hayden pregnant, I love seeing her stomach stretched with life inside of it.

"Yes. It's early on. I got the results on this paper the doctor gave me," she says waving the crumpled, forgotten paper in her hand. "I'm just a little over a month, but the doctor said everything looked fine."

"You're pregnant," I repeat again like a fool as the fact settles inside of me.

"I am. You think you can handle adding one more into our happy family?" she asks, and she looks happy, but I can see the fear she's trying to hide. She's nervous about this.

I open my hand on my lap. "Give me your hand, Beauty." She lays the paper down, then opens her hand against mine. "As long as you're in my life, I'm ready for anything. I can handle anything," I tell her in complete honestly. "I love our family and I'll love any child we're given in the future. There's nowhere on earth I'd rather be," I vow and I see the tears begin to form in the corner of her eye. I hate to see her cry, but these are okay. These are happy tears, because the happiness practically radiates from her. Connor's little chubby hand picks that moment to flop down on top of ours.

"Da' Da', Mo-mom!" he yells, and it's almost loud enough to drown out Hayden's gasp of surprise—but not quite. I look down at our three hands, joined together and combined by circumstance, by sorrow and pain, by happiness and joy, but most of all...*by love.*

It's that moment I feel that warmth I haven't felt again since that day at the hospital when I almost pushed Hayden away and lost everything. It radiates all around me and my lungs are filled with the scent of strawberries.

Annabelle is here. She is always here with me.

I give one last look at our hands. I told Hayden once what she gave me, here is just proof of it all over again. Here in this room. There is nothing but beauty—

*And all of it is mine.*

# EPILOGUE

## ANNABELLE

*Four months later*

"Daddy will be okay now," I whisper looking up at my uncle. He's holding my hand as we look down at Daddy and his new family sitting on the deck and looking up at the stars.

"Yeah, munchkin. I think your Dad will be just fine now. You were a good girl to watch over him and help him you know. He's very proud of you."

"I know. Do you think he knows I'm still here? That I'm happy now?" I ask Uncle Briar. He got here awhile back. I was sure glad to see him. He seemed sad at first, but you can't be sad here long. After he found some of his old friends and discovered his Mom and sister were here he was better. I like spending time with him. When I got here I was lonely without my daddy, but they let me play with the stars. It's my most favoritest thing to do and it's why Uncle Briar and I are here tonight. I have something special I want to do...for Daddy—to show him I'm happy too.

"I think he does," Uncle Briar says, ruffling my hair.

"I'll still get to see him won't I, Uncle Briar? I want to watch my brothers grow and watch over them too," I whisper my fear. I like where I'm at, but I don't want to lose my Dad or my family now. I want to watch over them until they can come be with me. Here time doesn't mean much, so I know soon I'll be able to hug them—even Hayden! I like her. She's a good mommy. That day at the house she whispered she loved me. I said it back, but she couldn't hear me.

"Nothing will change," he assures me and he's grinning. Uncle Briar grins a lot now.

"Good because big sisters are supposed to look out for their little brothers," I tell him. "And my new baby brother isn't born yet. He'll need me to watch over him extra!"

"That he will munchkin. That he will. Are you ready for the surprise you wanted to give your Dad?"

"Yep. I'm ready," I tell him.

I look out over the stars and I concentrate really hard. I giggle almost as loud as Uncle Briar laughs when the first stars shoot from the sky. I watch Hayden point it out to Dad.

"Michael look! It's a shooting star!" Hayden cries.

"I see it," Daddy says, standing up to hug Hayden close as they stare up at the sky together. Daddy is holding Connor and Hayden has her hand on her stomach where my new brother is resting. He'll be here soon. They're smiling and happy and Uncle Briar winks at me. I concentrate again and 2 more stars follow the path of the first, and then another and another. I make the sparkle extra so their path down reminds you of fireworks.

"We have to make a wish now for sure," Hayden laughs.

"You go ahead, Beauty. I have everything I want," Daddy says and it feels like he's looking at me when he looks up at the sky. Then his words float to me.

"Thank you Annabelle. Daddy loves you sweet baby girl," he whispers and I picture myself hugging him. I make sure he knows I'm there. He always thinks of strawberries with me and I make the air thick with the scent.

*I can do that now. I can do so much.*

Uncle Briar takes my hand and we slowly walk away.

*Daddy liked my surprise. I can tell by the way his laughter fills the night and follows me.*

*The End*

# A NOTE FROM THE AUTHOR

Dear Readers:

I hope you enjoyed Beauty and Beast's tale. This one I took my time on and I'm kind of proud of it. Normally I would leave you with an excerpt of my upcoming book. However, my next book will be Happy Trail which comes out no later than July. It's a Romantic Comedy series that started with Perfect Stroke and Raging Heart On. It didn't seem right to include a chapter of it. My next MC series will either be Devil's story or Diesel's and since I never know which voice will scream louder—I held off. You can always subscribe to my webpage and get updates or send me a note!

As always, I am ever grateful for your continued support. You allowed me to live my dream, and I am in your debt. You readers blow me away with your notes. I read each one personally and usually cry over them. Thank you from the bottom of my heart.

I haven't done this in what seems like way too long. To my "street" team—Jordan's Badass Bitches. You girls are so special. I love each of you and appreciate you so much. You give to me, always take time out of your day to make me smile and that support is priceless. Thank you. Meeting some of you has been the highlight of this whole author gig. I can't wait to meet more of you and see some of you again!

Martha Lanham even when you feel your worst, you reach out to try and help me. I love you lady!

My amazing Pimp Squad! Hah! Neringa Neringiukas, Whynter Raven, Jamie Grandison, Robin Yatsko, Veronica Garcia, and Robin Corcoran you make me cry. (And crap I hope I didn't leave any out, if I did Facebook hid you from me so feel free to slap me!) I love you! Thank you for taking the time out of your busy lives to share my books on social media and always—ALWAYS, making me smile.

I'd also like to shout out to Rose Holub, Danielle Palumbo, Michelle McGinty, Sheila Karr, Pauline Digaletos, Crystal Radaker, Paula May, Jenn Hazen, Tami Czenkus, and Jenna Gentzler Strick-houser for helping me find errors when I was so pressed for time. Life hasn't been easy this past month with Mom and I was so scared of disappointing the readers. Thank you for rallying around me. I love you all tremendously.

I'd like to give a special shout out to Amy Jones. You share my work constantly and you're always buying my books when you know that I would give them to you in a heartbeat. I don't know how to explain what your loyalty means to me. You've had such a hard time I know. I'm so tickled that you finally have something to celebrate in being an Aunt. I keep you close in my heart and prayers. Thank you for being my friend, and I feel in my heart that your mom is watching through the stars down on you—and smiling.

On that note, Dessure Hutchins there are no words to give you my thanks. You are my sanity when the world is killing me. My friend when I feel alone, and without you I'm not sure I could keep writing some days. You always make it fun, you keep it real

and you do it out of love, but I love you moistest. I love you—
bigger than a shark swimming in the sky.

xoxo

Jordan

**Read More Jordan With These Titles:**

# BOOKS LISTED BY SERIES

**Savage Brothers MC**
Breaking Dragon
Saving Dancer
Loving Nicole
Claiming Crusher
Trusting Bull
Needing Carrie

**Devil's Blaze MC**
Captured
Burned
Craved (Novella)
Released
Shafted
Beast
Beauty

**Lucas Brothers Series**
Perfect Stroke
Raging Heart On

# LINKS:

Here are my social media links! Make sure you sign up for my newsletter. I give things away there and you get to see things before others! I also have a blog on my webpage you can subscribe to and besides my strange ramblings I'll update you on my work in progress and give you delicious secrets.... or boring ones! One of those!

**Webpage Subscriber's Link:**
    https://www.jordanmarieromance.com/subscribe

**Facebook Page:**
    https://www.facebook.com/JordanMarieAuthor

**Twitter:**
    https://twitter.com/Author_JordanM
    Webpage:
    **Webpage**

LINKS:

http://jordanmarieromance.com

**Instagram:**
https://www.instagram.com/jordan_marie_author/
**Pinterest:**
https://www.pinterest.com/jordanmarieauth/

CPSIA information can be obtained
at www.ICGtesting.com
Printed in the USA
LVOW10s0421180418
573917LV00022B/900/P